Outcast

Loki's Exile: Book 2

J.C. DIEM

Copyright © 2017 J.C. DIEM

All rights reserved. Published by Seize The Night Publishing Agency.

No part of this publication may be reproduced or transmitted in any form or by any means, electronic or mechanical, including photocopying, recording, storage in an information retrieval system, or otherwise, without the prior written permission of the author.

ISBN-13: 978-1975827489
ISBN-10: 1975827481

This is a work of fiction. Names, characters, places, incidents and dialogues are products of the author's imagination or are used fictitiously. Any resemblance to actual people, living or dead, events or locales is entirely coincidental.

Titles by J.C. Diem:

Mortis Series
Death Beckons
Death Embraces
Death Deceives
Death Devours
Death Betrays
Death Banishes
Death Returns
Death Conquers
Death Reigns

Shifter Squad Series
Seven Psychics
Zombie King
Dark Coven
Rogue Wolf
Corpse Thieves
Snake Charmer
Vampire Matriarch
Web Master
Hell Spawn

Hellscourge Series
Road To Hell
To Hell And Back
Hell Bound
Hell Bent
Hell To Pay
Hell Freezes Over
Hell Raiser
Hell Hath No Fury
All Hell Breaks Loose

Fate's Warriors Trilogy
God Of Mischief
God Of Mayhem
God Of Malice

Loki's Exile Series
Exiled
Outcast
Forsaken
Destined

Hunter Elite Series
Hunting The Past
Hunting The Truth
Hunting A Master
Hunting For Death
Hunting A Thief
Hunting A Necromancer
Hunting A Relic
Hunting The Dark
Hunting A Dragon

Half Fae Hunter Series
Dark Moon Rising
Deadly Seduction
Dungeon Trials
Dragon Pledge

Unseelie Queen

Chapter One

Slowly awakening from an extremely vivid dream of a world where the cities weren't in ruins and people were plentiful, Bianca tried to hold onto the images for as long as she could. It had been so real that it was almost as if she'd lived another life for a short time. Reality became hard to ignore when she rolled onto her back and became aware of the hard ground beneath her. The animal furs she used for a mattress were barely adequate to cushion her.

An image lingered longer than the others as her dream began to fade. A tall man with a handsome face, shoulder-length black hair and bright blue eyes held her captivated. Then he dissipated along with the rest of her dream, leaving her feeling strangely bereft. "Get a hold of yourself," she said and gave up on trying to sleep. She sensed dawn would arrive soon, which meant it was nearly time to get up anyway.

It was pitch black, but she knew the cave well. Her clothes lay beside her makeshift bed in a tidy pile. She removed her threadbare t-shirt and pulled the worn outfit on. Leather was hot to wear in the middle of summer, but it was the hardiest material. It tended to last longer than anything else that she scrounged from the ruins of Reaverton. It was edging towards winter now, so the outfit was more bearable.

Next, she slipped on a belt that held sheaths with twin daggers on each side. The blades were long and thin, with fairly short handles and wide hilts with sharp points that could be used to maim and kill. The correct name for them was a Sai, or so her mentor had told her. She usually just called them daggers. At only five-foot-two, the sheaths were almost too long for her short legs. She strapped them to her thighs so they wouldn't get in the way when she had to run. Finally, she pulled on fingerless leather gloves that reached halfway up her wrists. They would protect her hands and arms from damage if she ran into trouble.

In the dark, she rummaged around in her backpack in search of food. Pale dawn light began to filter into the cave while she was chewing some dried meat for breakfast. For a moment, she could almost taste the fresh, delicious food from her weird dream. Then the final remnants dissipated and she forgot about the dream altogether.

Now that there was enough light to see, Bianca crossed to her one and only friend and companion. Mack was sitting on the chest where she'd left him before she'd gone to sleep. His single button eye stared sightlessly at her as she picked him up. She'd found the monkey six years ago, during her first foray into the ruins that had almost been her death. He'd been lying beneath a bunch of filthy, torn plush animals in an old toy store. His red shorts and blue t-shirt had caught her eye and she'd plucked him from the pile. Apart from his missing eye, he'd been intact.

Despite her mentor's frown, she'd stuffed the monkey into her pack. The cheerful grin embroidered on the toy's cute face had perked her spirits up. Tran Li hadn't told her to leave the toy behind. Maybe he'd figured she needed some joy in her life after the ordeal she'd barely survived.

Her brows drew down as a fresh stab of grief hit her. Tran Li had saved her life many times since he'd first rescued her. He'd taught her how to fight and how to stay alive. In return, she'd tried not to annoy him too much by pestering him with questions about his past.

Opening the chest, she draped Mack over her shoulder and crouched down to rummage around inside. Picking up a small book she'd found a few years ago and had filled with drawings, she flicked through it and stopped when she found a picture of her mentor. His dark eyes were slightly slanted and as inscrutable as ever. He'd rarely spoken and never smiled. His past had been as tragic as hers, what little she'd learned about him during five years of living with him.

Bianca realized a year had passed since his death. She sent a small surge of forbidden magic into Mack to animate him so she would have someone to talk to. Even though there was no one here to witness her antics, she still felt guilty about using her power. The monkey sat up and looked at her expectantly. "We should go visit Tran Li's grave," she said to her friend. He wrapped his long tail around her neck for balance and clapped his hands together, grinning in agreement. His movements were startlingly lifelike. "I knew you'd like the idea," she said and tickled him under his chin. He playfully batted her hand away and silently shook a finger to scold her.

It had taken her years to master her ability to animate things. The larger the object was, the harder it was to bring them to a semblance of life. Like the few other people who remained on her world, Tran Li had been afraid of magical power, so she hadn't practiced it in front of him. Now that he was gone, animating Mack was the only thing that was keeping her sane. Without his companionship, she'd probably have gone nuts months ago. Even though she'd been ostracized for years before she'd been exiled, at least there had been other people around. Being on her own was harder than she'd thought it would be.

In order to pay respects to her mentor, she would risk leaving her home for a short time. It was dangerous to venture outside during the day, but not as perilous as going out at night. The dull silver droids and gray clones had hunted humanity almost to extinction. They tended to stick to the cities where their masters had stationed them.

In the vast wastelands of Texas, the deadliest things were rattlesnakes. Tran Li had taught her how to keep watch for them and how to hunt them for food. They were tasty enough, not that she had much to compare it to. Before she'd been cast out of her original home, coyote, snake and lizard meat had been her main food source. Tran Li had found some vegetables after careful foraging and had created a small garden. It sat atop the cave and she tended it daily.

Mack poked her in the cheek with his furry hand, getting her attention when he realized her mind had wandered. With the garden in mind, she made her way through the tunnels to the underground spring. She had to tend to her duties before she could visit the graveyard.

Her mentor had lived here alone for a year before he'd found her. He'd drilled small holes in the tunnel ceilings to let in the light to illuminate the way to the small underground spring and various exits. She'd long ago grown accustomed to the dim light of her home.

Bianca knelt beside the small pool and used a metal cup to drink some of the cool, sweet water. She then filled a bucket and carried it to the nearest exit. It was tricky to climb up the rickety wooden ladder while carrying the bucket, but she managed it despite her small size. Mack leaped off her shoulder and scampered ahead, lightening her load slightly. She opened the trapdoor a crack and peered outside. Apart from a whirling dust devil, there was no sound, or movement. The mini tornado danced to an inaudible tune, scooping up dirt and flinging it around with abandon before suddenly collapsing.

Pushing the trapdoor open, she crouched in the shade of the boulders and waited until Mack scrambled back up to her shoulder before she closed the door again. Tran Li had cleverly disguised all of the entrances like this. He'd attached dirt and rocks to the openings, hiding them well.

With Mack clinging to her, she climbed to the top of a small cliff. The garden was hidden in a shallow depression that was shaded by an overhanging rock. It received enough light for the plants to thrive without being boiled to death by the harsh sunlight. She poured the water over the garden, making sure to get every single vegetable. Without fresh greens, she would become weak and grow sick. Her mentor had drummed that into her along with the other survival skills that he'd passed on to her.

Remaining in a crouch, Bianca raised a hand to shield her eyes from the early morning sun. The ruins of Reaverton glimmered far in the distance. Once a bustling city long ago, it looked like the carcass of a gigantic beast to her. She'd only been to the ruins a handful of times. Each foray had been frightening and fraught with peril.

Even decades after the invasion, clones still haunted the derelict buildings. At least they only hunted at night and couldn't come out during the day. They had a deadly allergy to the sun. The droids never slept and were always on the prowl. It was rumored that they'd once been fast and almost stealthy. Now they were rundown and wheezed noisily when they moved. Their weapons made up for their lack of speed. Their large, square guns turned humans into gray-skinned monsters. Their smaller weapons could disintegrate most types of metal, stone and flesh once they were changed to the correct setting.

Shuddering in dread, Bianca looked away from the place she'd vowed never to return to again. Her mentor had lost his life to the creatures that roamed Reaverton. He'd been missing for three nights before she'd finally forced herself to go in search of him. She'd found what was left of his body after following a bloody trail. The clones must have ambushed him somehow. They'd eaten most of him, leaving only his head and a few bones behind.

Bianca had found the supplies that he'd dropped before fleeing. She'd used a sheet of leather he'd scavenged to gather up his remains. She'd carried him to the closest abandoned town near their cave. It was an hour away on foot and had a small cemetery. She'd buried him there among the bodies of people who had died long before the world had been invaded.

Still shielding her eyes from the glare, she studied the small town. Nothing moved in the dusty streets. Not that she could see from here anyway. The cemetery was only a short distance away from the settlement. "It looks clear," she said and Mack nodded in agreement. Her strange magic imbued him with a semblance of life, which meant he could see and hear. If he'd had a proper mouth instead of just an embroidered line, she wondered if he would have been able to make sounds as well.

Shrugging off her curiosity, she returned to her cave long enough to put the bucket back in place and to grab a few supplies. With her worn backpack slung over one shoulder and Mack perched on the other, she climbed up the ladder again and emerged into the sunlight.

Chapter Two

Sweat trickled down Bianca's spine by the time she reached the cemetery. She'd gathered a few hardy wildflowers along the way. According to one of the books she'd found, leaving flowers on graves was a tradition a lot of people used to follow on the anniversary of a loved one's death. The posy was small and pitiful, but she didn't think Tran Li would mind. He would know she'd meant well.

Kneeling beside his grave, she lay the flowers in the shade of the crude headstone she'd made. It was just a small boulder that she'd carved his name onto, but it was better than nothing.

Mack patted her on the shoulder as her grief swelled. "I miss you," she said softly. "I wish you were still with me." Loneliness plucked at her with restless hands. She saw her solitary future stretching ahead of her and her shoulders sagged. Exiled by her own kind, no one wanted anything to do with a witch like her. She'd been cast out for her magical abilities. If she ever tried to return to the cavern where she'd been born, they would kill her. She was doomed to spend the rest of her life alone.

Tilting her head backwards in despair, Bianca's mouth dropped open when she saw a hole appear in the sky high above her. A person fell through, shooting a short blast of what looked like magic from his hands at something she couldn't see. The hole in the sky disappeared and the man fell. From his limpness, it looked like he'd fallen unconscious.

Instinct kicked in and Bianca went on the move. The sheet of leather she'd used to haul Tran Li's remains here lay where she'd left it a year ago. She grasped hold of it and held it out to a statue of a stone angel that watched over a grave. Withdrawing her power from Mack, the monkey became inert and fell to the ground. She sent a surge of power into the angel and it came to life. Its fingers closed around the edge of the sheet and Bianca took a few steps backwards. She lifted the material up just in time to catch the man.

His weight yanked her down to her knees and he rolled towards her. She barely had time to brace herself before she was knocked onto her back. The stranger lay on top of her with his cheek resting on her chest. Bianca looked at the angel to see her arching her brows in apparent disapproval. "Some help?" she croaked. Her wind had almost been knocked out of her by his heavy weight and she was feeling breathless.

Tilting her head to the side, the angel bent down and grasped hold of the stranger by his arms. She gently dragged him off her and rolled him onto his back. He was dressed in a green shirt and brown trousers that didn't smell particularly fresh. A fetid odor clung to them and his clothes were damp. His skin was pale and his black hair reached his shoulders. It was his face that held Bianca transfixed. He was easily the most handsome man she'd ever seen. He was also strangely familiar.

Acting on instinct again, she thumbed one of his eyelids open. Just as she'd somehow known, his eyes were a bright and dazzling blue. "Who are you?" she murmured. Unconscious, he didn't answer her.

Even though he was lying down, it was obvious he was a lot taller than she was. She wasn't going to be able to carry him back to her cave. Staying here wasn't an option. The people from her old underground village sometimes sent scouts out to scavenge for metal and other items. Her cave was the only safe place for her to hide.

Tran Li would have rolled over in his grave if he'd known what she was contemplating. Not only was she thinking of bringing a strange man to her home, he was also a magic user. "Which means he's an outcast, just like me," she said. That decided her and she searched for something that could offer her some help.

The angel rolled her eyes and shook her head in despair, apparently aware of what Bianca was planning to do. Bianca withdrew her magic and the statue returned to its original position. The lower half of the statue was a solid block, so the angel wouldn't be of any more use to her. She needed something with legs that would be large and strong enough to carry a tall man.

Her gaze came to rest on twin panthers that guarded the gates to the cemetery. Sitting on their haunches, they were life-sized, so they might be adequate to suit her purposes. Ancient and weathered, one was missing a front paw. The other had four intact paws. She sent power into it and it came to life. Swiveling its head, it saw her and let out a loud purr. It pranced over and rubbed against her, almost knocking her over. "Nice kitty," she said and patted it on its stony head.

Beneath her mental directions, the panther walked over to the unconscious man and came to a stop. Bianca wasn't strong enough to haul his dead weight onto the animal. She withdrew her power from the feline and poured it back into the angel. Becoming reanimated, she made a sound of disapproval, but she didn't say anything. Maybe she wasn't capable of speech.

Bianca didn't need to voice what she wanted her minion to do, she just had to think it. The angel bent and picked the stranger up and lay him facedown over the panther. The stone beast stood taller than her waist, but the man's feet dragged on the ground. "There's not much I can do about that," Bianca said with a shrug. She was already feeling tired from using her magic. She wouldn't be able to last the entire hour it would take to walk back to the cave at a normal pace while animating the stone animal. This meant she would have to get there a lot faster.

Scooping Mack up, she put him in her backpack. Taking a flask out of the pack, she took a long drink of water. Using a lot of power always drained her and this was going to push her to her limits. She ate some dried meat, had another drink, then put her supplies away. With the backpack over both shoulders, she climbed onto the stone cat and settled behind the unconscious stranger. Withdrawing her magic from the angel, she reanimated the panther again. "Take us home," she instructed the beast out loud. With a roar, it leaped into action.

Bianca held onto the stranger with both hands to keep him from falling off. She was exhilarated and terrified as the feline jumped over the fence and bounded across the arid soil. She fleetingly wished Tran Li was still alive to see this, then her focus went to holding on and to not losing her magic.

A vulture circled overhead, watching them avidly. If they fell from the beast and became badly injured, it would no doubt call more of its brethren to the feast that would ensue. While she could use her magic to bring objects to quasi-life, she couldn't heal herself, or others.

Chapter Three

Loki's head was pounding and his stomach felt like it was about to rebel. It didn't help that he appeared to be lying face-down over a galloping horse. Groggy and feeling decidedly ill, he moved his hands and feet slightly and was relieved to find they weren't bound. He opened his eyes and saw the ground was far too close to his face. In fact, his feet hit the soil each time the far too short animal bounded forward. He frowned, wondering what sort of horse bounded rather than galloped.

Placing his hands against the beast's side for balance, his frown deepened when he found the animal to be cold and hard. Only now did he realize it didn't sound like it had hooves. Whatever this thing was, it clearly wasn't a horse at all.

His feet hit the ground again and he raised them a little to lessen the impact. He became aware of hands pressed against the small of his back and realized he wasn't alone. He turned his head just enough to see a woman riding the strange beast behind him. His breath caught in his throat at her beauty.

For a moment, she seemed almost familiar. Her eyes were hazel, with strong hints of green. Her skin was tanned and freckles were speckled across her nose. High cheekbones and full lips gave her a natural loveliness that most women would kill for. Almost shoulder-length auburn hair framed her face. It appeared to have been cut by a blind person with a blunt knife, but the choppy, uneven look somehow suited her.

Unaware that she was being watched, she scanned the area as if searching for danger. He didn't know where he was and only vaguely remembered falling through a portal towards what he thought would be his death. Turning the other way, he tried to determine what sort of creature he and his mysterious savior were riding. As if sensing his scrutiny, the beast flicked a look at him over its shoulder. Shock coursed through him when he recognized it as a panther. It was highly realistic, for something that was made out of gray stone.

A wave of dizziness swept over him and he fought not to throw up. He wasn't sure how much more of this wild, punishing ride he could take. At that thought, the animal skidded to a stop. The girl slid gracefully to the ground, then the beast tossed Loki off. He landed on his back and his wind was knocked out of him.

His small companion opened a cleverly disguised trapdoor in the ground, then looked at him appraisingly. His eyes were only open a sliver and she didn't realize he was conscious. With his air trapped in his lungs, he didn't have the ability to speak, so he just lay there, wondering what she was going to do next.

Her tanned face had gone pale and her eyes were growing glassy. She reeled a little and seemed to be on the edge of exhaustion. When she glanced at the panther, it seemed to obey a mental command and slunk over to a group of boulders. It lay down next to them, curled into a ball and became inanimate. Only close examination would reveal its existence now.

Loki thought the girl was going to abandon him when she slipped into the hole in the ground. He was still fighting to get his breath back and to gather his strength. She returned a short while later carrying a length of rope over her narrow shoulder. To his astonishment, it came alive in her hands. She tossed it onto his chest and it wrapped around his upper body snugly.

Slithering across the ground, it dragged him over to the opening. The girl took him by the legs and swung him around so he was feet first, then knelt behind him. She grabbed hold of him and maneuvered him towards the opening. Even in his weak and ill state, he enjoyed the sensation of her lush breasts pressing against him. Since he wasn't sure he would have been able to descend the ladder himself, he remained silent and limp as the rope worked him towards the ground.

He travelled about twenty feet before his feet touched the bottom. The rope lowered him down until he was lying on his back. Loki looked up to see the girl descending towards him. He enjoyed the view of her shapely legs and backside encased in worn, tattered black leather until she lowered the trapdoor, plunging them into darkness.

His night vision kicked in as the rope dragged him through narrow, twisting tunnels to a large cave. Strategically placed holes in the ceiling gave enough light for him to see it was a living, sleeping and cooking area. His attention was drawn back to the girl as she stumbled into the cavern. She was breathing heavily and was tottering on her feet. The rope went slack as her eyes fluttered shut. He lurched to his feet and managed to catch her as she passed out from apparent exhaustion.

Too ill and unsteady to hold even her slight weight, Loki sank back to the ground. He cradled the girl's head on his lap and examined her. Several strands of auburn hair had fallen across her face. He brushed them away and frowned at the warmth that holding her brought him. There was no logical reason why she seemed so familiar. He'd never met her before and had never been to this place. "Who are you?" he murmured, but received no response. She was out cold and was beyond the ability to answer him.

Resting for a few minutes, he took his savior into his arms and staggered to his feet. He strode over to the crude bed and knelt to lay her down. She curled onto her side and he disentangled the backpack from her. Spying a flask inside, he opened it and smelled water. He drank thirstily and the liquid helped drive away his lingering sickness.

Sitting beside the girl, he leaned against the cave wall and searched the backpack more thoroughly. Apart from what looked like some dried meat and a toy monkey, there wasn't much to see. A stone to sharpen the weapons she wore on her hips was the only other item. Feeling hungry, he gingerly tried the meat and found it to be palatable enough. Taking the toy out, he sat it next to the girl. It stared at him with one button eye and almost seemed to be watching him suspiciously.

His strength slowly returned as he snacked and sipped water. Curious about this place, he saw a battered old chest and heaved himself to his feet. He crouched in front of it and opened the lid. A few books were stacked neatly to one side and a pile of clothing was on the other.

The book on top was a notepad. He flipped through it to see detailed drawings of places and people. A boy had been drawn a couple of times. He was handsome, but something was slightly off about his intense stare. A third image of the boy had been scribbled over so hard that the page had torn. An older man with slightly slanted eyes also featured several times, along with other ordinary looking people. The few buildings she'd drawn were badly damaged and looked like they'd suffered through a war.

Neither the notepad, nor the books gave him any sense of the name of the world he'd fallen into. Although it was arid and inhospitable so far, at least he hadn't been confronted with ugly green aliens who tried to poison him to death.

Putting the notebook back, he closed the chest and crossed to the girl again. He didn't know how, but he was certain that she'd saved his life. Not even he could have survived a fall from so high. He should have splattered to death in the graveyard he'd been falling towards when he'd passed out.

Rolling her onto her back, he shifted her so her head was lying on his lap. She gave a small, contended sigh and the strange warmth spilled into him again, leaving him feeling confused. Clearly, she possessed magic of some kind. Perhaps she also had the ability to bewitch him. If so, he would have to keep his guard up so she didn't ensnare him completely.

Chapter Four

A hand was running through Bianca's hair. The sensation was soothing, but strange. It had been a very long time since anyone had shown her any affection. She could vaguely remember her mother hugging her when she'd been small. Everything had changed with her death.

The hand shifted away from her hair and a finger softly stroked her cheek. Snapping awake, Bianca rolled to her feet and reached for her daggers. She had them pressed against the throat of the man who had been touching her before she remembered that she'd brought him here.

Loki went stock still when his companion moved with shocking speed. She knelt on either side of his legs. Her sharp daggers pricked his throat and her face was only inches away from his. Her eyes cleared as she blinked a few times. He noted that the green was more prominent now. "Who are you?" she asked in a low, menacing tone that perversely sent a jolt of raw lust straight through him.

"I am Loki, of Asgard," he replied.

"Ass Guard?" Bianca said with a frown. "I've never heard of it."

"Have we had this conversation before?" Loki asked. He almost lifted a hand to his head in confusion, but her daggers dug into his skin and he went still again. "This seems very familiar," he added with a charming smile. "My home is called *As*gard. Not Ass Guard."

"I've still never heard of it," Bianca said flatly. "And we've never met before. I saw you fall from the sky and I know you can use magic." She stared into his eyes, noting his confusion and disorientation. "Why are you here?"

"I fled from some hideous green aliens who tried to poison me," he replied. "Might I know your name?"

"I'm Bianca Caldwell." She waited for him to run screaming, but he didn't react to her infamous surname at all.

"What world am I on?"

The strange question threw her. "What do you mean? We're on Earth, of course."

"Earth?" His brow wrinkled, then smoothed out as he realized what language they were speaking. It had changed considerably since he'd last been here, but he still recognized it to be English. "You mean Midgard. Humans are calling it Earth now? That isn't exactly an inspired name."

"Humans?" Bianca said, sitting back on her haunches and pulling her daggers away from his throat. "Exactly where is this *As*gard place?"

Loki lounged against the cave wall and smirked. "It is a planet that is far away from here."

"How did you get here? Who were the aliens who attacked you?"

Now that she was no longer threatening his life, he took in the rest of her outfit. Her top was made of a combination of black and brown leather and had seen better days. It was sleeveless, with straps cinching in her waist and emphasizing her truly spectacular breasts. Not that they were overly large. They just seemed so because she was otherwise so petite. Her pants were tight and had several rips that revealed her far paler skin.

Bianca's stomach clenched in alarm when Loki's gaze strayed to her chest. No one had looked at her with desire for six years, but she recognized the glint in his eyes. She cleared her throat pointedly and his attention returned to her face again. He smiled winningly and she gave him a narrow, unimpressed stare.

Realizing he couldn't charm his way past ogling Bianca's assets, Loki replayed her question in his head and answered it. "I was exiled from Asgard by my King," he told her. "His henchman sent me to another world along a pathway called the bifrost. I ended up in a dismal, swampy world and was soon surrounded by its denizens. They attacked me without provocation, but I managed to escape from them. I found a small village and saw some silver contraptions that appeared to be windows to other worlds. I somehow infused one with magic after the aliens found me, then fell through it when they attacked me."

"It became a portal to this world?" Bianca asked. One of the few books she possessed dealt with mythical beings and portals to other dimensions.

"I assume so," he said, inclining his head. "May I ask why you are living in a cave?"

She stood and moved away to distance herself from him. She wasn't used to having company anymore and he made her nervous. "Most people live in caves now, since the ruins are too dangerous to approach. I used to live in a far larger cavern, but I was cast out six years ago. They were afraid of my magic."

From the haunted look in her eyes, it had been a traumatic experience. Her eyes darkened to a stormy gray, apparently from sadness. "You would have been very young at the time," he said in sympathy. Usually, he wouldn't have cared about the long-ago plight of a stranger, but he felt a strange kinship with her. They'd both been deemed as unworthy and had been exiled by their own people.

"I was fourteen," Bianca said in a husky voice, trying to hold onto her emotions. The events that had led to her being kicked out were still fresh in her mind. She shied away from the horrors she'd endured before she could become upset. Strange things happened when her emotions got the better of her.

"What happened to cause you to be cast out?" Loki asked softly. For a moment, her eyes almost looked dark brown as she seemed to become angry, but it had to be a trick of the dim light. No one's eyes changed color that fast.

"I don't talk about it," she replied flatly. "That's in the past and there's no point rehashing it."

It sounded like something she'd convinced herself of to protect her mind, so he didn't press her. "Have you been living alone in this cave for the past six years?" he asked.

"No. My mentor, Tran Li, also lived here." Bianca swallowed down her sadness, knowing her eyes would betray her emotions as they always did. "He was killed by the clones a year ago. That's why I was in the cemetery today. I went to visit his grave and saw you falling from a hole in the sky."

"You saved me?" he said with a brow raised. She nodded, confirming his hunch. "How?" He already knew about her magical abilities, so she described how she'd used a sheet of leather to catch him. Shaking his head, he had one more question for her. "Why did you catch me?"

Hesitating, she shifted uneasily. "I don't know. It was instinct."

"Well, I am very grateful that your instinct was to rescue me," he said with a sunny smile. "Now, can you explain what these clones are that you spoke of and how they killed your friend?"

This was a story Bianca didn't relish telling. Loki was a stranger to this world and he knew nothing of its dire history. "Would you like some tea?" she asked to stall him.

"I would, thank you." He knew she was putting off her tale, but that she would tell him when she was ready.

Tran Li had shown Bianca how to make tea from the few surviving native plants that grew in the desert. The brew was bitter, but drinkable. Leaving Loki, she trudged to the spring to fill the old kettle with water. She returned and settled next to the campfire and grabbed the kit to make a flame.

"Allow me," Loki said and pointed at the coals. They flared to life, making her start in surprise. "Fire was the first magic I learned how to wield," he said with a charming smile.

Tearing her eyes away from his far too handsome face, Bianca picked up a metal canister and plucked out some leaves. She put them in the kettle and set it over the flames. It took a few minutes to boil, then she poured them both a cup and set the kettle aside. She left the fire to burn, which gave them more light to see each other.

Knowing she couldn't put it off any longer, Bianca took a deep breath, then filled Loki in on the suffering that her world had endured.

Chapter Five

"Earth was normal once," she said, relaying the history she'd learned as a young child before her mother had died and everyone had shunned her. "There was always strife somewhere, but there were few wars and most people were relatively peaceful. Then, a few decades ago, we were invaded by aliens called Viltarans." Her tone became artic as she named the culprits who had ruined her planet.

"They came in a gigantic black spaceship and attacked a city called Los Angeles first," she went on. "They had tens of thousands of robots and strange little gray monsters to round up the populace. The robots used guns to shoot yellow darts at people to turn them into tall, gray monsters with red eyes. Each gun created identical creatures, but there were several slightly different versions. The survivors took to calling them clones."

She took a short break to sip some tea and Loki remained silent, simply watching her. "Shortly after the Viltarans invaded us, a woman tried to oppose them," Bianca continued. "She could use elemental magic and she was the only hope we had." She fell silent long enough for her companion to prompt her to continue.

"What happened?" Loki asked in a hushed tone.

"She failed," Bianca said with a shrug. "Her husband was killed by the leader of the Viltarans and she fell apart. She allowed our world to be ruined because of her grief. That's why I was exiled from my old home when they discovered I could use magic. It's because of her that witches are hated."

She hunched her shoulders and wrapped her arms around her legs. "I take it your magic was only discovered when you were a teenager?" he asked.

"Yes," Bianca said and took another sip of tea. "I paid the price for Whitney Caldwell's failure." Her tone was as bitter as the brew she was drinking.

Loki's gaze sharpened at the witch's surname. "I take it she is your ancestor?" Apparently, children took on their mother's surnames on this world.

"She was my great-grandmother," she confirmed with an unhappy smile that didn't reach her eyes. "She was pregnant when this all happened and died a few years after giving birth to a girl."

"Was her daughter also a witch?" Loki queried and noted her flinch at the term.

"No. I'm the first of her descendants to be able to use magic."

"When did you first learn that you were a sorceress?"

"When I was seven."

From her cool tone, she wasn't going to divulge more about her past to him just yet. "Someone eventually found out, hence why you were exiled," he surmised.

"I was supposed to die, but Tran Li rescued me," she told him. "He brought me here and taught me how to fight and how to survive."

"He didn't mind that you could use magic?"

Her expression became rueful. "He was just as afraid of it as everyone else. I practiced when I was alone." She glanced at the toy monkey and he came to life. He scampered over to her and climbed up onto her shoulder. His tail curled around her neck and his single eye went to Loki and glared at him suspiciously. "His name is Mack," she said.

"Mack the monkey," Loki said with a grin. "It suits him. What do you call the panther we rode to get here?"

She froze in the act of taking a sip of tea and stared at him. "You were awake during that ride?"

"Only towards the end," he admitted. "I was still recovering from being poisoned and I wasn't completely conscious."

Red stained her cheeks. "Were you awake when I used the rope to get you down the ladder?"

"Yes," he said and his smile widened. "The sensation of your breasts pressed up against my back is a moment that I shall cherish forever."

Her color increased, then she realized he was just teasing her. She sent him a withering look and he chuckled. He took a swig of tea, then grimaced at the taste. Clearly, he was used to far better food and beverages than anything she could supply. His gaze slid to her chest and back up to her face. His wink sent a flare of heat through her. The last time a man had been sexually interested in her, she'd come very close to dying. She wasn't about to allow that to happen again. One thing that ran in her family was tragedy when it came to men. Unlike her ancestors, she wasn't going to let a man become her ruin.

Loki's amusement faded when Bianca's eyes turned dark brown again. This time, he couldn't deny the unusual change in color. It lingered for a while before she shook her head and her tenseness faded.

"Getting back to this planet's history," she said in a cool tone, "it took the Viltarans over a year to subvert the population. They used toxic gas to pen the civilians in the cities while they unleashed their droids and clones. After they'd converted, or captured enough humans to suit their purposes, they gassed the entire planet. It dissipated over time, but it killed most of the people, plants and animals. This part of Texas was already a desert, but the rest of Earth is almost as bad now, or so I've heard."

"How many people survived?" Loki asked.

"Only a small fraction managed to flee underground in time. The cavern I used to live in only had about fifty people living in it." She had no way of knowing how many there were now.

He shook his head at the fate that had befallen humanity. "Are the Viltarans still here?"

"No. They left after they wiped most of us out." She'd seen a picture in an ancient newspaper of one of the aliens in Reaverton once. The Viltarans were even uglier than their clones.

"Yet, they left some of their minions behind."

It wasn't a question, but she nodded anyway. "They left some of their droids and clones in most cities all over the world to clean up any survivors who fled underground."

"How many ships did they have?" He needed to find a way back to Asgard and these aliens were probably his only hope.

"Just one big one, but they used a lot of small ones to carry their captives to the mothership. It hovered high over the cities as they were invaded, but it was apparently invisible so no one could shoot it out of the sky." Jets and other vehicles were a thing of the past, but the tales had been passed down from generation to generation.

Loki's lips thinned in disappointment. Even if they'd left any of their spacecrafts behind, it was doubtful a small transport ship would be able to carry him very far. "How am I going to get home?" he asked in near despair.

"They kicked you out," she reminded him. "Why would you even want to return to Asgard?"

"Because that is where I belong. I can't spend the rest of my lengthy life living on an almost uninhabitable planet that is nearly devoid of life." He looked around the cave with a sneer that he probably wasn't even aware of. "I don't relish living in squalor forever."

Taking offense at his haughty tone, Bianca stood and glared down at him. "I'm sorry my home isn't up to your usual standards, your Lordship," she said acerbically, then stalked off down a dark tunnel.

Realizing he'd offended her, he hurried to follow her, but she managed to keep ahead of him. Mack swiveled around on her shoulder and raised his tiny little fist in silent anger. Loki had to fight to suppress a bark of laughter at the animal's antics. Bianca had saved his life and he'd repaid her kindness by insulting her home. She deserved better treatment than this.

Sadly, he wasn't used to being nice, unless it was while trying to persuade a woman into his bed. It had been a very long time since he'd bothered to seduce a female. With the memory of Bianca's exceptional breasts pressed against him, he wasn't sure he would be able to resist her beauty for long.

Chapter Six

Muttering to herself, Bianca made her way to the spring and knelt to wash her metal cup out. When she stood and turned, Loki was right in front of her. She took a step back and tripped over a stone, but his hands shot out to catch her by the shoulders.

Staring down at Bianca, Loki realized she barely came up to his chest. She was so tiny that she made him feel huge and oafish. "You are very small," he observed.

"You're very tall," she shot back and shrugged his hands off. Her palms came to rest on her weapons warningly, reminding him of the speed she'd used earlier. From the way her daggers had pricked his skin, her magic could break through his shields that should have kept him safe. Maybe his power didn't work quite as well here.

He backed up a step and she took his cup, then knelt and washed it. "I am sorry for offending you," he said. "I guess I have become spoiled from living on Asgard."

"What's your world like?" she asked.

"It's beautiful," he replied wistfully. He'd only been exiled a short while ago, yet he missed it as if he'd been gone for more than a year. "It has golden cities, vast forests, mountains that are perpetually covered in snow and countless lakes."

"It sounds like paradise. I hear Earth used to be the same."

"I remember. The last time I was here, things were very different."

"You've been here before?"

"A very long time ago."

She studied him, but couldn't determine his age. She was about to ask, but before she could, Mack's head swiveled around and he peered down the dim tunnel. "What is it?" she asked. His small face contorted into an expression of fear and he pointed at the tunnel that led to the exit. The shuffling of feet trying to be stealthy reached them and her hands went to her daggers. "They've found us," she said and turned to run.

"Who are you speaking about?" Loki asked as he raced after her. She might be short, but she could move very quickly.

"The people from my old cave," she replied, then sprinted for the exit. If they were caught, they would both die horribly. This time, Tran Li wouldn't be there to rescue her.

She reached the ladder and began to climb. Pausing at the top, she checked that the way was clear before climbing out and crouching beside the boulders. Shouts came from inside the cave and at the base of the cliff. They were surrounded and it was only a matter of time before they would be caught.

Loki climbed out and lowered the trapdoor, then looked at Bianca with a raised brow. "What now?" he asked. "Do we fight, or run?"

"There's too many of them for us to fight," she replied. Her tone was almost clinical, but her eyes were verging on green, belying her fear. "If we stay, we'll die. If we try to run, they'll catch us."

"And then we'll die?" he said dryly.

"Exactly," she said with a complete lack of humor.

"Then, perhaps it is time I showed these people who I really am," Loki said and stood. He held his hands out dramatically, but something hit him in the back of the head before he could finish whatever he'd been about to do.

Bianca lurched forward to catch him as he fell to his knees, knocked out cold. Looking over his shoulder, she saw Craig, the leader of her old cavern smirking down at her. Short and stocky, he had red hair and cold brown eyes. He'd waited for them to be flushed out by his people before springing his trap.

"This time, you'll face justice, witch," he said with a sneer that she'd seen a thousand times before. He hurled another rock and she didn't have time to dodge it. It hit her in the temple and she joined Loki in unconsciousness.

Loki's head was pounding again when he woke. He had a moment of déjà vu to find himself being carried. This time, he wasn't lying face-down over the back of a stone panther. Instead, he'd been tied to a crude stretcher. He opened his eyes a sliver to see four burly men hauling him. Behind them, Bianca had also been strapped to a stretcher and was being carried by two men. She was limp and unconscious and her pet monkey was nowhere to be seen. Rage flared inside him, but he decided to bide his time before retaliating. His personal shield had gone on the fritz and had failed him twice now. He wasn't sure how much of his magic would work here. His real clothing was still concealed, so he guessed his illusion spell was holding.

These people had cast Bianca out and he suspected her eviction from their settlement hadn't been pleasant. Instead of simply killing them both, they'd decided to capture them. That didn't bode well for their future.

Their captors had unkempt hair, dirty faces and worn, patched clothing mostly in shades of brown. Their eyes darted around fearfully, searching for threats. Lean to the point of emaciation, they looked like they were barely surviving in this harsh environment. Now that Bianca's cave had been discovered, they would no doubt claim it as their own. The natural spring would be too precious for them to ignore.

Shadows fell over them as they entered a narrow gorge between two cliffs. True darkness descended as he was carried into a tunnel. They didn't need light to make their way along the well-worn path to a gigantic cavern. Flaming torches and firepits illuminated the area. Women and children gathered in small groups, staring at the captives in hostility. One of the older women spat in Bianca's direction, but she was too far away for the projectile to land on her. "Filthy magic using whore," she muttered.

Again, Loki's rage flared. He barely knew Bianca, but he was offended on her behalf. How dare these people treat her so badly? They should be revering her for her talents that set her apart from them rather than punishing her for being different.

He was carried over to the wall and was propped up at an angle. He let his head hang forward, pretending to be unconscious. Bianca was propped up beside him. Blood matted her hair on her temple and ran down to her jaw. His rage simmered just beneath the surface to see her wounded. He felt protective of her without fully understanding why. Maybe it was because she was so small and fragile

Leaving them leaning against the wall, the warriors gathered around their leader. Loki used a small amount of magic to listen in on their conversation and was glad when his trick worked. Maybe only his shields were affected.

"Did you kill Tran Li?" their leader asked.

One of the men shook his head. "He wasn't in the cave and there was no sign of him. It looks like she was living alone."

"Who is he then?" the leader said, jerking his head towards Loki.

"He's the man I saw her carrying on the back of the stone beast early this morning," another warrior said.

Loki cursed himself silently. If Bianca hadn't saved him and brought him to her home, they wouldn't have found her. She'd endangered herself by rescuing him and now she was paying the price for it.

"Where did he come from?" the leader asked.

"I don't know," the warrior shrugged. "I just saw the two of them racing across the desert and followed the tracks to her cave."

"He could be innocent, Craig," another warrior said doubtfully. "He might not know she's a witch."

"It doesn't matter," Craig said dismissively. "She's already bewitched him by now. He'll be her creature, just like Tran Li and Sean were." Loki lifted his head fractionally to see them looking at a young man who was crouched next to a fire. He was staring fixedly at Bianca's slumbering form. Loki recognized him from the drawing in the notepad. He was older now, but he was still a good-looking kid. Jealousy twisted his insides. Clearly, Bianca had a history with him. He didn't like the possessive way the boy was staring at her.

"What are we going to do with them?" a warrior asked.

Craig stared at the captives for a long moment before responding. "We will do what we'd planned to do to the witch six years ago before Tran Li rescued her from her fate. We will sacrifice them both to the gods."

Breaths were indrawn by most of the warriors. "You mean we'll be taking her to Reaverton again?" the bravest man said in a bare whisper.

Their leader's face was cold and his smile was wintry when he responded. "Ready the horses," he responded. "We leave in ten minutes."

Chapter Seven

Bianca opened her eyes and immediately shut them again when harsh sunlight stung her retinas. A strange rumbling sound drowned out all other noise. Her temple was throbbing in pain and her whole body ached. She lay on something hard that seemed to be moving. It took her a moment to realize the rumbling sound was wheels. She was tied down and was being transported on a cart.

Loki knew the instant Bianca woke. Her entire body went tense, but she didn't make a sound. They were lying side by side and he reached out with his pinky finger and touched her hand. She flinched and turned her head, then sagged in relief when she saw him. "I must say, the hospitality on your world has been sorely lacking so far," he said gravely. Her lips turned upwards in a small smile that quickly died. "Are you all right?" he asked her quietly.

"Not really," she replied truthfully. "How long have we been in the cart?"

"About two hours."

Lifting her head, she managed to peer over the side of the vehicle. Recognizing a distant pile of boulders to be her home, she reached out with her magic. She'd never tried to animate Mack from so far away before. He'd fallen from her shoulder at the top of the cliff next to the trapdoor. Sweat popped out on her brow as she tried to pour her magic into him. She felt a faint connection, then slumped in defeat as they moved too far away for her to try to control him.

"Did you reach Mack?" Loki asked, still speaking quietly. Three warriors rode at the front of the carriage. One flicked a suspicious glance over his shoulder, then turned away again. Tied down, the captives weren't going to be a danger, or so their captors erroneously assumed.

"He's too far away," Bianca replied. She couldn't hide her despair. A horrible sense of déjà vu flooded through her. Six years ago, she'd been in this exact position. She'd been betrayed and the entire cave had turned on her for being a witch. Craig had decided her fate was to be sacrificed back then. Now here she was again, on her way to the ruins she did her best to avoid.

"Do you have any idea what is going to happen to us?" Loki asked.

"I imagine we're being taken to Reaverton to be sacrificed to the 'gods'."

She'd unwittingly repeated Craig's words almost exactly. He heard the quotation marks in her tone and knew she didn't share their beliefs. "Reaverton?" he asked in near amusement. "Was this city named after actual pirates and outlaws?"

She managed a slight shrug. "I have no idea. We don't exactly have many history books left. The monsters that inhabit the ruins could almost pass for raiders, I guess, except they kill and eat people rather than rob and rape them."

"Is that the fate these men intend for us?" Loki said. "To be killed and eaten?"

"That's usually what happens. Tran Li saved me the last time. This time, we're on our own."

"How long will it take us to reach Reaverton?"

"Two days at this pace," she replied. "We'll arrive before nightfall tomorrow."

"You've been through this before." He studied her drawn face, needing to know more. "Who betrayed you the last time?"

"His name is Sean," she said bitterly, confirming his hunch about the handsome young man who had stared at her with such possessiveness. "He found out that I could use magic and betrayed me. I was captured and knocked out. They tied me up, transported me to Reaverton, then tied me to a pole just before sundown. They left me there for the clones and droids to find."

"Tran Li discovered you before the monsters and mechanical men arrived?"

"He saw me and cut me loose just as the clones woke up and went hunting. I was lucky that the droids were patrolling another section of the city." She shivered at the memory of the bestial roars that had echoed through the ruins. The tortured clanking of rusty metal feet had sounded, but they'd easily outrun the droids that had been heading their way.

"How did he die?"

"He went on a scavenging expedition and the clones must have caught him," she replied. "They ate everything except for his head."

He gagged slightly at the picture that conjured up. If he didn't do something, he and Bianca would share that same grisly fate. If he acted too soon, the cave dwellers who had captured them would continue to be a problem. "I have a plan," he said. "But you have to trust me."

Studying his face, he looked confident to the point of cockiness. "Do I have a choice?" Bianca asked wryly. She could have taken control of her ropes and turned them against their captors, but one of them was bound to kill her before she could get all three of them. She'd seen Loki use magic, but only as he'd fallen through the hole in the sky. Maybe he couldn't use it on her world. Whatever his plan was, she hoped it would keep them both alive.

Horses were rare and highly prized, so they stopped frequently to rest, feed and water the animals. Loki and Bianca were mostly ignored. Their jailers didn't care if they expired from thirst. While Bianca's skin was already tanned, Loki's skin burned badly beneath the relentless sun. His face blistered and peeled and his lips cracked and bled. He would have almost welcomed death by the time they finally reached the outskirts of the ruins. Every now and then, he saw a vulture circling overhead, judging how juicy a meal they would make. The feathers on its right wing were slightly ruffled and one stuck out at an awkward angle. It soared away and he lost sight of it.

The sun would set in an hour or so, which meant certain death would find them shortly afterwards. Two of the warriors hauled Loki out first while the third one held a knife ready to stab him if he tried to fight them. They dragged him over to a crude platform that sported several metal poles. He was tied firmly, then Bianca was carried over as well. She looked like a defenseless child between the two men. Even as lean as they were, they were far larger than she was.

Head swimming from exhaustion and thirst, Bianca half expected Tran Li to leap to her defense as she was tied to the metal pole. The shadows were growing long and the sun would soon depart from the sky. With frightened backward glances, the warriors scurried over to the cart and climbed on board. Flicking the reins, the driver forced the horses into a gallop. He wanted to put as much distance between himself and the ruins as he could.

Looking around, Loki saw broken buildings, rusted hunks of metal that had once been vehicles and human skeletons scattered around. "How lovely," he murmured. "Reaverton really lives up to its name."

Bianca spared him a glance, then attempted to muster up the strength to imbue her ropes with magic. She'd learned a lot during the past six years. It should have been child's play for her to bring the rope to life. Inexplicably tired, she was having trouble focusing. Seeing something scurrying towards them, she slumped in amazed relief when she realized it was Mack. He was dragging the backpack that she'd left in the cave behind him.

From Bianca's shocked expression, Loki figured she'd had no idea her pet monkey had come at her call.

"How did you get here?" she croaked.

Mack climbed up onto the platform and dropped the backpack next to her. He mimed waking up and slipping into the tunnels. He'd found the backpack, filled it with water and food and had then raced after the cart. He'd caught up to it and had apparently hitched a ride underneath. Bianca was tired because she hadn't withdrawn her magic from her friend. She'd been inadvertently powering him the entire time.

Opening the backpack, Mack held up one of the sheaths that had been stolen from her. He'd filched the daggers back from their captors while she and Loki had been transferred to the platform.

"You know, I'm beginning to warm up to that monkey," Loki said with a wide grin. It turned sickly and disappeared when he heard an unholy roar coming from somewhere within the ruins. "What was that?" he whispered.

"That was a clone," Bianca replied just as quietly. "We need to find shelter before they catch our scent."

Loki conjured up a small burst of fire and his ropes fell to the ground. Mack had clambered up to Bianca's waist and used the Sai to cut her free. Loki was a bit miffed that his grand plan to rescue them had been upstaged by a stuffed toy, but he kept his complaints to himself. Bianca hugged the animal before placing him on her shoulder. She took her dagger from him while he wrapped his tail around her neck for balance.

Mack wasn't really alive, but he was the only friend Bianca had. It would be far too dangerous to return to her cave now that it had been discovered by her enemies. He'd been just within range of her magic as she and Loki had been carried past her home. She was profoundly glad he'd managed to follow them and catch up to the cart to hitch a ride. Leaving him behind would have been devastating.

Taking a few moments to strap her sheaths in place, she found two flasks of water inside the backpack and handed one to Loki. "Take small sips," she warned him. He nodded and took her advice, trusting she knew how to survive in this hostile place far better than he did. His stomach cramped when the lukewarm water hit his insides. He waited for the pain to fade before taking another small drink.

"Let's go," Bianca said, taking charge.

He was surprised when she headed towards the ruins rather than away from them. "Isn't it dangerous for us to stay here?" he whispered.

She flicked a glance at him over her shoulder. "Yeah, but the clones will head into the desert to hunt. It'll be far more dangerous in the wasteland than it will be here. We'll only have the droids to worry about and we can hear them coming from a few blocks away."

He couldn't argue with that logic and followed her deeper into the city.

Chapter Eight

A thin sliver of a moon gave her just enough light to see where she was going as she cautiously made her way through the ruins. Piles of rubble from destroyed buildings blocked her way. She did her best to move around them rather than attempting to climb over them. Loki didn't strike her as the outdoors type. He muttered curses each time they had to scale an obstruction. It was lucky the clones went in search of food in the desert because he made enough noise to raise the dead.

Hearing heavy, clomping footsteps approaching, Bianca grabbed hold of Loki and crouched down behind the rusted hulk of a car. He hunkered beside her as they peered around the vehicle to see a robot emerge from a side street. About nine feet tall, it was made of dull silver, had a short, stubby nose and a mouth that was just a thin lipless opening. Scarlet eyes and pointed ears were the final touches. The Viltarans hadn't put a lot of effort into shaping their mechanical minions. A bulky contraption that was probably a computer was attached to its left wrist.

Holding a small device in its hand, it swept it from side to side and came to a stop pointing directly at them. Its head rose and it raised a large gun with a square barrel filled with dozens of projectiles.

"Run!" Bianca said in a hoarse whisper and shoved Loki into action. Bright yellow vials of fluid shot through the air after them. If even one of them pierced their flesh, they would be turned into clones and they'd become ravenous killing machines.

Loki raised an invisible magical shield that was large enough to cover them both. It seemed he had to concentrate to get his magic to work. He couldn't rely on it automatically saving him. The darts splattered harmlessly on the invisible barrier as they raced deeper into Reaverton. He followed Bianca as she descended a staircase that led down into darkness.

Bianca knew they would have a much better chance of survival in the bowels of the city. The scanners the droids used to find humans didn't work as well underground. With the clones currently searching for food, the subway was the safest place for them to be until dawn arrived. The only problem was that it was pitch black down here. As if reading her mind, a sword appeared at Loki's side and began to glow with silver light. "Where did that come from?" she asked, trying hard to hide her awe. His magic was very different from hers.

His expression became enigmatic. "I am a master of illusion, my dear," he said in an overly condescending tone that made her narrow her eyes slightly. "Once we are safe, I will reveal my true appearance to you."

"Gee, I can't wait," she said with a hint of sarcasm and continued to descend. The likelihood that they would ever be safe was slim.

Loki's sword gave them enough light to see maybe ten feet in all directions. She held both daggers ready, trusting Mack to warn them of any danger. Magically animated, his senses were far sharper than hers.

Silver trains stretched out into the darkness as they made their way along the platform. When it came to an end, they jumped down onto the tracks. Bones lay scattered for several yards, making their footing unsteady. Some were from animals, but most were human. Bianca barely spared them a glance as she stepped over them. Death haunted this planet and still sought new victims to torment. It would catch up to her one day, but she was going to do her best to escape it for as long as she could.

Leaving the bones behind, they passed several doors as they moved deeper into the tunnel. They were service entrances that the long dead employees had once used to access other parts of the subway.

They needed to find somewhere secure to hide, so Bianca chose a door at random. She tried the handle, but it was locked. Feeling Loki at her back, she was momentarily trapped between him and the door when he reached around her. She turned her head to look up at him over her shoulder. He smirked at her annoyed expression for encroaching on her space. The lock clicked as he used his magic to open it and he turned the handle. "After you," he invited her.

"Are you always this…" she trailed off, unable to think of a word to adequately describe him.

"Endearing?" he suggested with a grin.

"'Annoying' would be closer to the mark."

"That is a word that has been used to describe my unique personality on more than one occasion," he admitted. "On many worlds, I am known as the God of Mischief."

"You're a god?" she said with a disdainful look. "I find that very hard to believe."

Putting a hand over his heart, he put on a wounded look. "Are you always so quick to judge?"

"Yes," she said as she stepped into a narrow hallway. "On many worlds, I am known as the Mistress of Skepticism."

He laughed and shut the door, locking it again. "I can think of many titles that would suit you far better than that," he said silkily.

She held her hand up to stop him before he could form a list. "I don't even want to know," she said sourly. If he truly was a god, he had to be a minor one. A real god wouldn't have needed to be saved by a mere mortal after falling through a portal in the sky.

Loki couldn't contain his grin as he followed her along the hallway. Despite the danger they were in, he hadn't had this much fun in decades. After two centuries of being mostly abstinent, he'd finally found a woman who stimulated more than just his libido. Bianca was beautiful, tough and intelligent. She would have made an excellent Valkyrie on Asgard. Somehow, he could see her with golden wings and a sword in her hand.

Feeling the weight of Loki's stare on her back, Bianca refused to turn around and face him. He was an enigma that she didn't think could ever be solved. He'd dropped out of the sky and into her life and she'd felt compelled to save him. Now she was being hunted by humans, droids and clones. He wasn't from her world and he didn't belong here. The strange connection she felt with him wasn't real. It had been born of stress and the instinct to survive. Once they managed to escape from Reaverton, they would part ways and he wouldn't be her problem anymore.

They reached a set of stairs and headed upwards. Loki used his magic to unlock the door at the top. Mack leaned forward, poked his head out to check for danger, then waved them onward. They were on another platform that was deep in the heart of the city. From the number of bones strewn about, this was another nest for the clones.

Wrinkling her nose at the rank smell of rotting meat, Bianca hurried across the platform to another door. Loki followed closely on her heels. He opened the door and locked it behind them when they were on the other side. They descended the stairs to find the passage ahead was blocked by rubble.

Several books lay on the ground. They were a rare commodity and Bianca knelt and picked one up. It was moldy and unreadable, so she put it back down again. Water had seeped in from somewhere and the hallway was damp. She looked up and saw a narrow crack above her. It was too dark to see what was up there.

Loki lifted his sword up to shed some light into the room above. "It appears to be a library," he said. "It is set below the ground, so it should be safe from the droids." Lowering his sword, he waited for her verdict on what they should do.

"We have to stay somewhere until dawn," Bianca conceded. She'd read about libraries in her books, but had never imagined she would ever see one. The gap in the concrete was just wide enough for them to squeeze through. Rusty metal bars were threaded through the concrete. Some were sharp enough to cause a serious injury if they weren't careful.

"Up you go," Loki said and sheathed his sword. He put his hands on her waist and lifted her up to the fissure. She climbed upwards and glared when he put his hand on her shapely backside to give her a boost. He gave her an innocent look in return.

Shaking her head at Loki's inability to remain serious, Bianca didn't attempt to help him climb up to the opening. He was far too heavy and he would only pull her back down again. She moved aside as he leaped upwards. He caught hold of the jagged edge and easily pulled himself inside.

Mack rolled his eye when the Asgardian posed as if he was expecting applause for his acrobatics. Bianca crossed her arms and sniffed, clearly unimpressed. "Find something to cover the hole so we don't fall through it," she said. With that command, she wandered over to the nearest bookshelf.

Disconcerted to be ordered about, Loki opened his mouth to issue a retort. Mack's head swiveled towards him and looked at him knowingly. Closing his mouth again, Loki realized there was nothing he could say that wouldn't make him look like an ass. Muttering beneath his breath, he searched the room and found an overturned table with a broken leg. He tore the remaining legs off and carried the thick wooden tabletop over to the hole.

"Nice work," Bianca said and he mentally shook his head at the small glow he felt at her grudging praise. He was feeling more and more drawn to her, but it would be folly to let any emotions develop between them. She was a mere mortal and her lifespan would be over in the blink of an eye. But that didn't mean they couldn't enjoy each other while he was on her world.

Noting Loki's sly smirk, Bianca returned to perusing the bookshelves. She didn't know what his agenda was. Trusting him would be stupid. They might share the ability to use magic, but that didn't mean he had her best interests at heart. He gave her the distinct impression that his first and only concern would always be for himself.

Chapter Nine

"I'm starving," Loki complained when the silence stretched out. "What supplies did your little friend pack for us?"

Well-used to going without food, Bianca was able to ignore her hunger pains. She'd learned to ration her meals a long time ago. Loki was used to being pampered and had probably never known true hunger before. She tossed him the backpack and he caught it deftly. "That's all the food we have," she warned him. "Eat sparingly."

He saluted her sarcastically, silently conceding that she was right. He found some dried meat and bit off a piece. He tossed the rest to her and Mack snatched it out of the air and handed it to her. She patted him in thanks and Loki felt another flare of jealousy. He ruefully acknowledged it had been far too long since he'd been with a woman. He'd become fixated on Bianca and wanted her badly. Even her pet monkey was a rival to him.

Chewing the stringy lump of meat, he decided to explore the library. He left Lævateinn propped up against an overturned chair so it could illuminate the center of the room. With a flick of his hands, he sent shining globes of pure white light up to the ceiling high overhead.

Bianca gasped in wonder when the globes hung suspended in the air. Loki's smile was smug and she had the sense that he was showing off. She'd been the only witch in existence for her entire life. It was strange to finally meet another magic user. His power far surpassed hers. It exhausted her to simply animate one object for long. Loki seemed to have an unlimited supply of magic.

Now that there was so much more light, she didn't need to strain to read the titles of the books. Most were ruined by the damp that had permeated the room. The smell of putrid water hung in the air. Mold darkened the ancient carpet in several areas and it was spongy beneath her feet.

Loki searched for books on ancient mythology and came across an entire shelf of tomes. His brow furrowed when he found no mention of Asgard at all among the Norse mythology books. It seemed Bianca wasn't the only one who had never heard of his home. That added weight to his theory that he was in a different dimension. If he'd already existed in this realm, he wouldn't have been able to travel here. Asgard and its people may have been destroyed sometime in the distant past.

"What's wrong?" Bianca asked when she saw Loki frown deeply.

"You mean apart from us ruthlessly being hunted by robots and monsters?" he said dryly. "It would seem the portal that I fell through has taken me further away from my home than I'd realized."

"What do you mean?" she asked and abandoned her search to cross to him.

"I can find no mention of Asgard in any of these books," he replied, sweeping his hand over the shelves.

"No one here has heard of Ass Guard at all? How is that possible?"

"It's *As*gard," he corrected her in a mock stern tone. "I suspect my people no longer exist in this dimension."

Her brows rose at that implication. "There's more than one dimension?"

"Oh, yes," he said in an off-hand tone. "There are many realms and copies of ourselves on most."

"Can we travel to a dimension where we already exist?"

"No. It would create a paradox."

She'd never heard the word before, but grasped its implications. "How are you going to return to your reality?"

His shoulders sagged a little at the question that had been burning in his mind ever since he'd arrived here. "I don't know," he replied softly. Lifting a finger to the hair that had matted on her temple, he brushed it away to examine the cut on her forehead. "That looks nasty. I'd better tend to it."

"Can you heal injuries?" she asked, wide-eyed with wonder.

He slanted her a regretful smile and shook his head. "Alas, that is not one of my talents." He led her over to the backpack and they sat next to the sword so he could see her wound clearly.

"What talents to you have?" she asked and regretted it immediately when he grinned lecherously.

"They are many and varied," he said and chuckled at her annoyance. "When it comes to magic, illusion and destructive spells are my area of expertise." He could repair objects that had been destroyed, but at great cost. Fixing living flesh was beyond him.

He delved into the backpack and withdrew a piece of cloth. It was old and raggedy and had probably once been a washcloth. It was clean enough, so he moistened a corner and motioned for Bianca to move closer. She shuffled over and sat still while he washed the blood away. "I wish I had a healing salve," he muttered. The cut was narrow, but deep. The rock had left a bruise that had to be almost as painful as the cut. "Who is responsible for injuring us?" he asked. His back had been turned to the culprit when he'd been knocked out.

"His name is Craig," Bianca replied. "He's their leader."

"He will pay for this," Loki vowed, unsurprised by her answer. His own head was still throbbing in pain from where he'd been hit by a rock.

"It wouldn't be wise to seek revenge," she pointed out. "They probably think we're dead by now. I'd prefer it if they continued to believe that so I don't have to look over my shoulder constantly."

It went against his instincts to let his vengeance lie, but he nodded in agreement. "There," he declared when her wound was clean. "Hopefully, it will not become infected."

Infection was something every remaining human worried about. A couple of years ago, Tran Li had gotten a cut on his finger that had turned bad. He'd chopped the tip of his finger off and had cauterized the wound with fire to prevent the infection from spreading. Shuddering inwardly, she motioned for Loki to turn around. "Let me see how bad your wound is."

He could have told her he was fine, but he obeyed her command. She was so small that she had to raise up on her knees to reach him. Her fingers worked their way into his hair until they met his scalp. With far more gentleness than he'd expected, she found the lump on the back of his head. He closed his eyes at the sensation of her breath on the back of his neck as she searched for any cuts.

"You'll be fine," Bianca said and her breath caught in her throat when Loki looked over his shoulder. His blue eyes blazed with desire. If he was this affected by her mere touch, she wondered how he would react if she dared to kiss him.

For a long moment, Loki lived in hope that Bianca would brush her mouth against his. Instead, her face went blank and she pulled away. When Sean had betrayed her after learning she could use magic, he'd shattered something inside her. She'd lost the ability to trust her emotions.

He silently vowed that he would prove to her that not all men were untrustworthy. Repeating that thought in his head, he wanted to slap himself. He barely knew her, yet he couldn't shake the feeling that they'd met before. He felt a connection to her that shouldn't even exist. It was almost as if they'd been fated to meet.

Turning away from Loki, Bianca took a small sip of water and attempted to school her expression to neutrality. He evoked feelings in her that she'd never encountered before. If what he'd told her was true, then he was a demi-god. She didn't need to read a book about mythology to tell her that gods and mortals didn't mix.

Chapter Ten

Needing a break from Loki's intense stare, Bianca explored the rest of the library. Without her needing to ask, Loki created a new globe and attached it to Mack's back. The monkey glared at him over his shoulder. Bianca laughed, then seemed almost surprised by the sound, as if it was a rare occurrence. It made Loki sad that she'd known so little joy in her young life.

He headed in the opposite direction, using his sword to light his way. The library was extensive and he worked his way through several rooms. He located a couple of exits, but both were blocked by rubble. He found a bathroom and one of the taps dripped water. Putting his hand beneath the liquid, he bent to drink. Something landed on his back, making him jerk in alarm and the water splashed back into the sink.

"I wouldn't drink that if I were you," Bianca warned him.

Mack scampered onto Loki's shoulder and his tail wrapped snugly around his neck. The animated toy pointed at the tap and shook his head in warning. Loki wasn't sure if Bianca was directing him, or if he was acting on his own. "What's wrong with it?" he asked.

"Can't you smell it?" she asked and wrinkled her nose.

"This entire planet smells bad to me," he confessed.

"The droids poisoned the water after their masters left. They took their orders to kill the survivors seriously."

Wiping his hand on his trousers, he was very glad she'd turned up in time. "It would appear you have saved my life again."

"I'll try not to make a habit of it," she replied. She studied him by the combined light of his sword and the globe on Mack's back. He might not be able to heal himself, but his sunburn was already fading. His skin had stopped peeling and the redness was fading. His lips weren't as cracked now.

"Is there something wrong with my face?" Loki asked with a brow raised knowingly.

"You heal a lot quicker than I do. Your sunburn doesn't seem anywhere near as bad now."

"It's one of the perks of being a god," he said smugly as she left the room and they returned to the main area. Mack seemed comfortable hitching a ride with him and his tail wasn't too tight around his neck. He decided to leave the animal in place rather than shooing the creature away. Taking the globe from the animal's back, he casually tossed it into the air. It settled above them, nestled among the other lights.

"Tell me about your people," Bianca said when they settled on a mold free spot on the floor. He propped his sword against the chair and doused the silver glow until they just had the soft light from the globes above them to see by. "Can everyone on your planet use magic?"

"No," he said with a wry smile. "Asgardian men pride themselves on their prowess in battle. Sorcery is considered to be almost womanly."

From his unhappy smile, she figured it was a sore point. "So, you're stronger in magic than you are in combat?"

He delved into a belt that appeared from out of nowhere and plucked several daggers from it. With a flick of his wrist, he sent them flying across the room to lodge in the spines of three different books. "I would not say that," he said modestly, then used telekinesis to draw the weapons back to his hand. "I am quite proficient at fighting, even though I am somewhat smaller than most of my kin."

"Smaller?" she said incredulously. "I find that hard to believe." Compared to her, he was a giant.

"I am sure you would change your mind about that if you ever met Thor," he said dryly.

"Who is he?" She had a feeling he was one of Loki's rivals.

"He is Asgard's greatest warrior. Humans call him the God of Thunder."

"Why?"

"He wields a hammer that can call lightening from the sky."

"Is that all the magic he can do?"

"Pretty much," he said with a shrug. "He is a one-trick pony, but lightning is a very effective tool. His prowess in battle is also quite impressive."

"Which means all the other warriors must fawn all over him," Bianca surmised.

He lifted a sardonic brow in agreement. "It is almost as though you've already met him," he said.

"What does he look like?"

"He is two inches taller than me and twice my size in muscle mass. He has a short beard, blond hair and blue eyes."

"Your people respect him even though he uses a magic hammer?"

Loki inclined his head. "Odin, our King, is Thor's father and he gifted the weapon to his son. Odin uses magic like I do, yet he is admired by all." He said that with a twist of his lips. "He is as much a sorcerer as he is a warrior, which is why his magic is tolerated."

"He's the one who exiled you," she recalled. "What did you do to get kicked off Asgard?"

"My mischievous nature is to blame," he said self-deprecatingly. "I saw an opportunity to overthrow him and stupidly took it." He briefly told her about overhearing a conversation between several traitorous warriors and the part he'd played in their scheme. "Odin dispelled my illusion and revealed my true identity to his court," he finished up. "Nobody was really surprised to learn that I was behind the assassination attempt. Even if I'd had a chance to defend myself, they would never have believed that I simply saw an opportunity and seized it. They believe I was responsible for the entire plan."

"I believe you," she said, surprising him by the way his head jerked towards her.

"You do? Why?"

"Organizing a coup would take a lot of work. I don't see you as someone who could be bothered with the nitty gritty details."

Her honesty was refreshing and he chuckled. "You barely know me, yet you already know me better than my own kin do."

"I wouldn't go that far," she said. "You just seem too spoiled to soil your hands with hard work to me."

Glancing down at his grimy hands, he smiled ruefully. "It would seem I have changed in the short time I've been here." Their eyes met and the air became charged. "I have you to thank for that," he added softly.

"People don't change," she said flatly. "We are who we are and nothing can alter it."

He wasn't so sure about that. Only a few days ago, he'd attempted to overthrow Odin. Now, he couldn't imagine what he'd been thinking. The desire to rule Asgard had bled away. Being on the run for his life was probably behind it. "Tell me about your mentor, Tran Li," he said.

Her smile was real this time and held a tinge of sadness. "I didn't even know he existed until after he saved my life. He'd lived in a cave in another part of Texas seven years ago. It was discovered by raiders and everyone was slaughtered. He'd been hunting at the time and came home to find everyone dead. He left and ended up in the cave where I took you. He found Craig's cavern before I came along and apparently traded with them from time to time." That had stopped after he'd rescued her from their attempt to sacrifice her. She'd never seen him before, so he hadn't entered their cave during his trading sessions.

"I take it his ancestors weren't native to this area?" Loki asked.

"No. They came from another country. Somewhere in Asia, he told me."

"I wonder why he didn't live in the cavern with you and your people?"

"They wouldn't have accepted him," she replied. "They're afraid of anyone who is different from them."

"They're idiots," he said. "They rejected two of the best warriors on this squalid planet for what reason? Superstition?"

"I'm not a warrior," she denied.

Loki didn't give her any warning before he launched himself at her. Grabbing hold of her shoulders, he pinned her to the ground. In a flash, she pulled a dagger and held it against his throat. Mack's tail tightened around his neck to the point of cutting off his air. "Are you sure about that?" he said, choking the words out. He let her go and sat back down. Mack's hold didn't loosen. His angry eye glared at Loki and he shook his tiny fist.

Realizing he'd just been making a point, Bianca sat up, sheathed her Sai and called Mack to her. The monkey settled on her shoulder and they both watched Loki warily. "Tran Li taught me how to defend myself," she said tightly. "That doesn't make me a warrior."

"Your ancestor was supposed to save this world," he said. She nodded hesitantly and he could tell the change of topic threw her. "Have you not wondered why you also possess magical abilities?"

Fiddling with a tear in her pants, Bianca looked away. "I've never really thought about it before. I hid my ability from everyone when I learned I could use magic."

"What about your parents? Didn't they know?"

"My mother never told me who my father is. She died a year before I learned I could use magic." Her grief at losing her mother had faded, but it had never really gone away. With Tran Li's death, she'd lost the only two people she'd ever cared about.

"I think you have been chosen," Loki said, jolting her out of her memories.

"Chosen by who?"

"Whomever it was who gave your great-grandmother the ability to use magic."

She looked at him as if he'd gone crazy. "She failed to save our world. It's beyond rescuing now."

"Perhaps your purpose isn't to save this planet." His stare was intense, but not from sexual tension this time. He had something else on his mind. "Perhaps you have a different purpose."

"Really?" she said suspiciously. "What is my purpose, then?"

He spread his hands out wide. "Why, to save me, of course."

She shared a look with Mack. The monkey was just as skeptical as she was about his theory. "Your ego must be enormous," she said. "Do you really think I've been given magic just so I could rescue you?"

"I do, actually," he said with a pleased smile. "Isn't it a bit of a coincidence that you just happened to be in the exact spot where I fell from the sky?" She frowned slightly at that irrefutable logic. "Out of all the places in this world for me to end up, it just happened to be directly above the one and only witch on this world?" Her frown deepened, but it did nothing to detract from her beauty. "I think you were intended to assist me," he finished up.

"Assist you with what?" she asked dourly. She didn't like the idea of being some unknown entity's pawn.

"With helping me find a way home, of course," he replied far too innocently, then smiled widely. He was sure there were a few other things she could assist him with as well. But he wisely kept that thought to himself.

Chapter Eleven

Feeling tired and unsettled by Loki's assumption that she'd been created to serve him, Bianca chose a relatively clean spot on the floor and lay down. He doused the magical globes until only a few remained. They hovered around the edges of the room, casting a dim light on them. Loki lay down a few feet away, carefully keeping his sword away from her. It was warded so only he could touch it and he didn't want her to get zapped.

Mack settled down beside Bianca, but she didn't withdraw her magic from him. Using it constantly for the past couple of days had exhausted her at first, but she was getting used to it. Maybe she was adjusting to the added strain. Her furry friend didn't need to sleep and he would be an effective sentry.

Sinking into a deep sleep, she woke sometime later when Mack prodded her in the side. She sat up and her movement woke Loki. They both heard a noise and Mack pointed at one of the doors that was blocked on the other side. Muffled metallic footsteps sounded, then violet light filtered through cracks in the door.

"Droids," Bianca whispered. "I don't know how they found us, but they're going to break in here at any moment." Their weapons could disintegrate most materials and it was only a matter of time before they cleared the rubble away.

"We need to leave," Loki said grimly and shifted the tabletop away from the gap in the floor. He grabbed hold of Mack by the legs and lowered him head-first into the opening. Hanging upside down, Mack looked around, then motioned that it was safe. He scampered up Loki's shoulder and wrapped his tail around his neck as the Asgardian slipped through the fissure and dropped to the hallway below.

Bianca quickly followed him. She tensed when he grabbed her around the legs, but she didn't protest. He held her while she slid the table back over the gap, then he lowered her to the ground. They heard heavy footsteps approaching from the far end of the hallway and realized they were about to become trapped.

"Quickly, in here," Loki whispered, pointing at a nearby doorway. He used his magic to unlock it and she followed him inside. He locked it again and they were plunged into darkness. "Do you trust me?" he asked. He could see well enough, but she blinked owlishly and held her hands out in front of her protectively.

Bianca shook her head. "Not really." She didn't know him well enough to trust him yet.

"I thought that might be your answer," he said with a sigh. "My night vision is excellent and I can navigate through the hallways easily. I'm going to use my magic to increase my speed."

"Off you go then," she said sourly and waved at the passageway she couldn't even see. "Don't mind me, I'm sure I'll be fine alone here with the droids once they break in."

"Don't be silly," he said and she sucked in a surprised gasp when he swept her into his arms. "I'm taking you with me, of course." Mustering his magic, he sped away as he heard the droids break into the main hallway behind them.

Bianca wrapped her arms around Loki's neck as they rushed along the pure black hallway. Mack clung to her hand while his tail stayed firmly around Loki's neck. He was either giving her comfort, or seeking it. She was terrified they were going to crash into something, but Loki's vision proved to be as good as he'd boasted. Each time they came to a door, he slowed down to unlock it, then took off again.

By the time he found a set of stairs leading to the surface, he was breathing hard. He would have to recharge after using that much magic in a short space of time. He put Bianca down and she immediately steered him towards a narrow alley. They crouched in the shadows as something large, gray and muscular slunk past the opening.

Loki shuddered at his first sight of a clone. It had been human once, but it was now eight feet tall, muscular and hideous. He caught a glimpse of its face and saw teeth that were more like tusks protruding from its mouth. It wore a tattered loincloth, but was otherwise naked.

They'd slept for a few hours before the droids had found them and it was almost dawn now. The clones were returning from their hunt and had to find shelter before the sun rose. They watched several more pass by, then one turned its head and saw them. Scarlet eyes widened in surprise, then flared brightly in instant hunger. It roared and the hairs on Loki's arms and on the back of his neck rose at its savagery.

Bianca went into motion before he could even think of blasting it with magic. She sprinted past him, drawing her daggers. Ducking under the clone's clumsy swing, she darted behind it and severed both its Achilles tendons with two swipes of her blades. The beast fell to its knees and she reached forward over its shoulders and sliced its throat open. Bright yellow blood sheeted down the creature's chest and it gurgled in agony as it fell onto its face.

Astonished by how fast she'd moved, Loki watched Bianca as she returned to him. Her eyes were flat and devoid of emotion as she impatiently motioned for him to stand. "We need to get out of here," she told him. "With luck, the clones will be distracted by the fresh corpse long enough for us to leave the ruins."

"They eat their own kind?" he asked as he rose and followed her down the alley.

She shot a sardonic look over her shoulder before replying. "They'll eat any sort of meat. They don't care where it comes from." She cleaned her daggers with a strip of cloth before putting them to rest in their sheaths.

Loki looked at Mack and the monkey gestured for him to hurry up. Shaking his head that he was following the orders of a plush toy, he hastened after his companion. They had to clamber over a pile of debris at the end of the alley. He looked back to see several hulking clones hunkering next to their fallen comrade. With wet tearing sounds, they pulled the dead monster apart. When it had been dismembered, they continued their journey to safety, clutching their spoils.

"What a charming world," Loki murmured sarcastically. The swampy planet he'd briefly been exiled to had been bad, but this was far worse. If Heimdall had been able to send him across dimensions, he probably would have chosen this exact realm for his punishment.

Metallic footsteps echoed through the streets, indicating that the droids were moving in to surround them. They were relentless in their pursuit and they wouldn't stop until their directives had been reached.

Their masters had ordered them to kill any humans they encountered and disobeying wasn't an option.

"We can outrun them and possibly lose them completely if we can find somewhere underground to hide," Bianca said as she guided Loki towards the edge of Reaverton. "But I'm not sure where we should go." They couldn't return to her cave and she didn't know of any other caverns in the area that would be safe for them.

Standing in the shadows of a derelict building, Loki peered at the landscape and saw what looked like the skeleton of a gigantic beast. Squinting at it, he realized his error. Whatever it was, it was manmade. "I see a large structure in the distance," he told her. "Perhaps it will offer us shelter."

"What does it look like?" she asked. Her eyesight wasn't as good as his.

"It appears to be made of metal and looks something like a prehistoric dinosaur."

"It's probably an old rig that was used to dig oil," she surmised. They were dotted all over Texas, but she'd never seen one up close. "I guess we don't have much choice but to check it out," she said. They couldn't stay here, that was for sure. She just hoped they would reach the old machinery before the sun fried them both to death.

Chapter Twelve

"Wait here for a minute," Bianca said to Loki. "I'm going to scavenge for some items." Before he could ask her what sort of objects she needed, she darted back into the ruins. Finding what had once been a clothing store, she made her way to the back where the pickings would be better. Sheltered from the elements, she found some denim jeans beneath a pile of tattered shirts. Even after all this time, they were still intact. Grabbing two pairs, she stuffed them into her backpack. Another destroyed store caught her eye on her way back and she hurried inside. It was an old arts and crafts store. She scrounged for some more items, then returned to Loki.

Mack bobbed up and down on the tall man's shoulder anxiously, pointing at the wasteland. He was urging them to leave. The clones had all returned to their nests, but the droids could march forever. They needed to get far enough ahead of them so they could find a hiding spot. That meant they had a long walk ahead and few supplies to keep them going.

"Let's go," Bianca said and took off at a fast walk.

Loki had little choice but to follow her. He knew he wouldn't survive for long on his own in this harsh environment. Her mentor had taught her how to live in the desert and now she was going to be his savior.

When the sun rose a short while later, sweat instantly popped up on his brow. Bianca stopped long enough to take the jeans out of her backpack. She handed a pair to him, then used one of her daggers to slice the legs off the other pair. She pulled them over her gloves up to her shoulders. The rest she fashioned into a small turban to shield her head.

With a fatalistic shrug, Loki wrapped the jeans around his head until it was covered. "What do you think?" he asked and posed for her. "Does it suit me?"

Bianca's lips pressed into a thin line, then she burst out laughing. The legs of the jeans dangled down each side of his head like deformed ears. "You look ridiculous," she said with a snigger. "But at least your scalp won't get burnt again."

They recommenced their trek and he was already thirsty. He judged it would take them a full twenty-four hours to reach the metallic relic. He wasn't sure he'd be able to make it that far in this heat with the little water they had.

Delving into her backpack, Bianca took out a needle, thread and a small black button. Mack looked at her, then pointed at his missing eye. "Yes," she replied to his unspoken question. "I finally found you a new eye." He clapped his hands in glee, then leaped over to her shoulder. Loki felt a little envious when the monkey moved around to her chest and nestled between her breasts. Mack didn't feel pain, so he made no protest when she poked the needle and thread into his face. Keeping one eye on the ground so she wouldn't trip, she quickly sewed the button on. "How's that?" she asked when she was done.

Mack swiveled his head from side to side, then clapped again. His mouth couldn't open, but he would have giggled if he'd been able to. With two eyes to see, he would be even more effective at helping them keep watch. He leaped back over to Loki, preferring to have a higher vantage point. His head turned in all directions as he searched for threats.

Bianca glanced at Loki an hour later to see how he was holding up. She was much shorter than he was, but she'd set a pace that he was struggling to keep up with. "Are you thirsty?" she asked.

"Of course," he replied. "Aren't you?" He'd resisted asking for a drink out of sheer pride. He didn't want her to think he was weak. In reality, his throat was dry and his tongue felt like a lump of rock.

He'd been tempted to snatch the backpack away from her more than once and drain both flasks dry.

"I'm used to it," she said. He wasn't, so she taught him a trick Tran Li had showed her long ago. Stopping at a cactus, she carefully sliced off a small branch. Cutting away the wickedly sharp spikes, she handed it to him. "Chew on that, but don't swallow the pulp," she instructed him. "It tastes bad, but the moisture will keep you alive."

Taking it gingerly, he put it in his mouth and winced at the taste. She was right, it did have a horrid flavor. The sensation of actual moisture made up for its nastiness. She cut off a piece for herself, then they recommenced their journey.

They chewed dried meat for breakfast and washed it down with a small sip of water. Their rations were already dangerously low, but Bianca wasn't worried. Texas had become a gigantic desert, but there was still life to be found. Overhead, a vulture soared past. It watched them for a while, then decided they weren't going to offer it a meal and flapped lazily away. Its right wing appeared to be damaged and she noticed that a feather stuck out strangely.

Lizards and snakes froze in fear when they sensed them approaching. They blended in with the arid soil, but she spotted them easily. There was plenty of food to be found, as long as she wasn't picky. Flicking a look at Loki, she wondered how he would feel if he knew the dried meat he was chewing had come from a rattlesnake.

Aware of Bianca's scrutiny, Loki gave her a sunny smile. "It's a lovely day for a stroll," he said drolly. "There's so much to see out here."

"Are you always this sarcastic?" She was genuinely curious to hear his answer.

"Yes," he replied easily. "It amuses me to confound people."

"I bet you've had a lot of practice at it."

"Centuries," he said with a grin.

She stared at him, unable to tell if he was lying. "Are you serious?"

"I am over a thousand years old," he said demurely.

"How long do Asgardians live?"

"Odin is five thousand or so," he said. "For us, that is quite ancient." Although the old coot was showing no signs of dying just yet.

"But, you can die?" she pressed.

"All things die eventually."

"I thought gods were immortal."

"Humans were the ones who called us gods," he said. "Compared to them, we are."

She rolled her eyes at his snobby tone. "Is it difficult?" she asked.

His brow furrowed in confusion. "Is what difficult?"

"Carrying that huge ego around," she clarified. "It must really weigh you down sometimes."

He sent her a sardonic look that was ruined by his badly fashioned denim hat. "You are impertinent," he declared, then his expression turned sly. "Fortunately for you, I find that trait adorable." Mack tightened his tail around Loki's neck fractionally in warning. "Did you make him do that?" Loki asked, using a finger to loosen the animal's hold.

"Do what?" Bianca asked.

"His tail tightened around my throat."

"Nope. He did it all on his own." She studied the toy, who was glaring at Loki. "Maybe he doesn't like it when you flirt with me."

"Don't you control his every action?"

"Mack is different from the other objects I've animated," she said, struggling to explain. "When I first found him on a scavenging trip in Reaverton, I had to direct all his movements. Over time, he started acting on his own accord. I think I've infused him with so much of my magic by now that he's become far more sentient than usual."

"Fascinating," Loki said. He lifted the monkey off his shoulder and held him with one hand. "Do you understand me?" he asked. Mack rolled his eyes and nodded grumpily. "Are you alive?" The monkey lifted a hand and waved it from side to side. "You need Bianca's magic to be able to operate?" Loki asked for clarification and the toy nodded again. "I wonder what would happen if I used my magic on you?"

Before Bianca could object, he sent a jolt of power into the toy. Blue light flared around Mack and he let out a screech through suddenly mobile lips. He clapped a hand over his mouth and blinked eyes that had become far more realistic.

"What did you do?" Bianca asked in alarm as she took her pet from him. While Mack still wasn't a flesh and blood animal, he'd changed. His face was far more monkey-like and his small body was shuddering in shock. He clung to her and stared at Loki reproachfully. He had a proper mouth with teeth rather than just an embroidered line now.

"I don't really know," Loki replied. "I just followed my instincts."

"Are you okay?" she asked Mack.

He nodded and made a chittering sound. He even had ears now and they shifted as he sniffed with his little brown nose. She withdrew her magic from him and he remained alert. She wasn't sure what Loki had done, but Mack no longer needed a constant flow of her magic to remain sentient. Exchanging looks of wonder, they continued on towards the distant relic.

Chapter Thirteen

After an excruciatingly long and hot day, darkness finally fell, bringing welcome coolness with it. A different type of animal made itself known and Loki started when a howl sounded from somewhere in the distance. "What was that?" he asked.

"It's just a coyote," Bianca replied. Her tone was unconcerned, which made him relax again. "They're not dangerous on their own, but a pack of them could become a problem."

"Are they edible?"

Her nose wrinkled, but she nodded. "They don't taste very good, but it's better than starving."

He was hungry enough not to be particular about what he ate. They didn't have much food and they needed to stock up. "Do you think we can catch one?"

Looking him up and down, she came to a stop. "I'll have a much better chance if I hunt them alone."

"I won't slow you down," he said stiffly.

"No offense, but you're still not used to this world," she said. "You might scare them away before I can get within a hundred yards of them."

Perched on his shoulder again, Mack nodded solemnly in agreement, then patted Loki on the shoulder in commiseration of his apparent unworthiness as a hunter. "Fine. I'll wait here then," he said sourly. He had far more experience hunting game than she did, but he was used to tracking animals on his world. He wasn't even sure what a coyote was yet.

Bianca felt a bit guilty for leaving him behind, but she frankly wanted some time on her own. Trotting away, she left Mack behind to keep his eye on her companion. Even the monkey had better survival skills than the Asgardian.

Following the yips and howls, she zeroed in on a small pack of coyotes. There was no wind to betray her scent to them as she crept up close. Spying a rat emerging from a hole in the ground, most of the pack took off after it. One hung back and became her target. Drawing a dagger, she whistled and the animal spun around to confront her. With a precise flick of her wrist, she sent the Sai flying toward her target. It landed in its neck, severing an artery.

The coyote fell with a small sound of pain. It would have bled to death within a few minutes, but she didn't believe in letting animals suffer. A swipe of her blade across its throat ended its life. Bianca hoisted it over her shoulder, being careful to hold its head away from her body so she wouldn't become soaked by the drops of blood that continued to drip from the carcass.

Loki was sitting on the ground when she returned to him. His upper lip wrinkled when she dumped the coyote near him. He pointed at it like it was a poisonous toad. "That is a dog," he said in disgust. "Do you really expect me to eat that?"

"I'm not going to force you to eat it, your Highness," she said dryly. "You can always stick to chewing cactus."

Removing the makeshift sleeves and gloves so her hands were bare, she increased his disgust by skinning the animal mere yards away from him. Her hands and arms were coated in blood by the time she was done. She didn't have any water to spare, so she rubbed dirt on her skin to clean most of the blood off. Loki's expression was bemused and almost horrified when she brushed the dirt off as best she could. "This is what life on this version of Earth is like," she said. "You either learn to adapt, or you die."

"Death might be preferable," he said in distaste. "Do you want me to cook that?" he asked, pointing at the butchered dog again.

"You can cook?" she asked in surprise.

"In a manner of speaking," he replied enigmatically, then conjured up fire. Using two fingers, he picked the carcass up and dropped it onto the flames. With some concentration, he was able to roast the coyote evenly rather than burning it to a crisp. It didn't smell particularly appetizing, but he was hungry enough that his mouth was watering by the time it was done. He let the fire die and they waited for it to cool slightly before slicing into the meat.

"It's not bad," Bianca said after taking a bite. Coyote meat was far from her favorite type of food, but she'd had worse.

"It's horrible," Loki argued with a sour face, but he finished off the hunk he'd carved for himself and reached for more.

Bianca quickly cut the meat into strips and Loki used more fire to dry them. Now they had enough food to last them for a week or so. They left the remains behind, knowing other predators would finish it off, then they continued their journey.

Walking through the night, they were exhausted by the time they neared the monolith that Loki had spotted from Reaverton. Up close, the hulk was impressive, but it looked like it would topple over at any time. A large triangular frame with a rickety ladder supported a massive metal beam. An oversized head made it look like a dinosaur from a distance was on one end of the beam. The other end was connected to the base. The head of the rig was linked to machinery that had enabled it to pump oil from the ground long ago. It was so rusted that it was inoperable, but he could see how it had worked.

Rectangular buildings with flat roofs were clustered together behind the rig. It was where the employees had presumably lived. There didn't seem to be any tunnels for them to descend into. Dawn was almost on them and they needed to be under cover before the sun could sap what was left of their reserves.

"Hopefully, the droids won't follow us this far," Bianca said, but her tone was doubtful. While the robots rarely strayed from the ruins, they'd been known to hunt their targets mercilessly once they had a human in their sights.

"What are the chances that these buildings are empty?" Loki asked. The few windows he saw were covered by ancient blinds so he couldn't see inside.

"There might be some coyotes living in there, but not much else would be this far from civilization." She made a dour face after saying that. Civilization had been left behind long ago when her planet had first been invaded. Now it was almost devoid of humans and all of the cities had been destroyed by Viltaran weaponry. The few survivors were downright savage at times. They had to be in order to stay alive.

Striding towards the short, plain buildings, Loki readied his sword. He was almost reeling from exhaustion by now and he just wanted to sleep. Bianca was weary as well, but held both daggers in her hands. He opened the door to the first dwelling and conjured up a ball of light. It lit the small space, revealing a decrepit table and chairs sitting in the middle of the room. Several bunkbeds lined the back wall and a tiny kitchenette was to the left.

"Actual beds," Loki said in mock amazement. He crossed to them and poked a mattress with his sword. Nothing scampered out from the stuffing, so he deemed it to be free of vermin.

Bianca crossed to another door at the back of the room. She opened it, listened briefly, then closed it again. "I think we'll be safe here, for a while at least," she said. They couldn't stay here forever, but they could rest for the day and recharge their batteries.

Choosing one of the lower bunks, she lay down and almost groaned in pleasure at lying on a real mattress. For a moment, the sensation of a comfortable bed almost seemed familiar, then the thought was gone as she fell asleep.

Loki didn't lie down immediately, even though he was wretchedly tired. The globe of light hovered near the ceiling in the middle of the room. It cast soft light over Bianca, highlighting the auburn in her hair. Her tan had deepened, almost hiding the freckles that spattered across her nose. He was disturbed by how attracted he was to her. There was something about her that called to him and he was finding it very hard to resist her allure.

Mack climbed up onto the table and turned to face him. He put his hands on his hips, staring at him with suspicious black eyes. With a soft laugh, Loki lay down on the barely adequate bed. His legs were too long, so he had to lie on his side and draw them up so his feet didn't dangle over the end. He'd never imagined he would be reduced to trusting a toy monkey to watch over him, but this entire world was crazy. Closing his eyes, he succumbed to sleep.

Chapter Fourteen

Bianca dreamt she was lying in a tub full of heated water. She'd never been fully submerged before, but it seemed strangely familiar and she luxuriated in the sensation of being clean. She became aware she wasn't alone when hands drew her back against a hard chest. Desire rose even before she tilted her head back to see Loki smirking down at her. His hair was wet and had been slicked back from his face. He winked and a flare of lust spiraled through her. His hands slid up her soapy torso to cup her breasts. Suddenly finding it hard to breathe, she sucked in air as he teased her nipples to peaks. "What are you doing to me?" she asked in a breathless voice.

"Hopefully giving you as much pleasure as I will receive," he replied silkily. His hands swept down her body to the juncture between her legs. He nudged them apart and she groaned when he rubbed her center. "Do you like that?" he asked, knowing the answer already.

"Yes," she moaned. "Don't stop."

"Oh, I won't, love," he replied with a chuckle that rumbled through her back. "I won't stop until you've been thoroughly satiated." He took her earlobe in his teeth and bit down gently before releasing her. "I am afraid this could take quite a while."

His hands continued to stroke, squeeze and torment her. She was on the edge of feeling the greatest pleasure she'd ever known when a noise woke her. "Damn it!" she groaned and sat up.

"Is something wrong?" Loki asked her innocently. From the faint moans she'd been making, she'd been having a very pleasant dream. Even in the dim light, he saw her eyes had gone a shade that was very close to blue. It was fascinating to watch them change color along with her emotions.

For a moment, she wondered if he'd somehow sent her that dream, then dismissed it as being highly unlikely. "What was that noise?" she asked, ignoring his question. She wasn't about to explain why she was so disappointed at being woken up.

Her moans had woken him, but he realized he'd faintly heard something else that must have woken her up. They turned to see Mack staring at the door warily. He flicked Bianca a worried look, then leaped over to her shoulder. He made quiet, frightened chittering noises and pointed at the door that led deeper into the building. It would hopefully take them to another exit.

"I think it might be a good idea for us to leave," she said, but her warning came too late. A clone burst inside and roared a challenge. Loki cursed and snatched up his sword. The creature smacked it out of his hand, then picked him up and threw him across the room. Mack launched himself at the clone and wrapped his tail around his throat. His small face was determined as he squeezed with all of his might.

Wheezing for air, the monster tried to pull the monkey away. Succeeding, it tossed the toy aside and started for Bianca. There wasn't much room to move, but she darted behind the table to slow it down. With one hand, it shoved the table aside and Bianca went into motion, calling on the training Tran Li had taught her. The clone had just woken up, so it was slower than usual. She avoided its grasp and darted in to stab it in the side. Bellowing in pain, it pushed her away. She slammed into the wall, then ducked when it tried to punch her. Its fist became stuck in the wall and she pulled her dagger free from its side. Trapped between her foe and the wall, she stabbed frantically with both weapons, puncturing its internal organs from its stomach all the way up to its chest.

Surging to his feet, Loki used his magic to propel himself across the room. He took hold of the monster and dragged it away from Bianca, but it was already dying. The beast fell, weakly trying to grab them even as it bled out. "These things are tenacious," he observed clinically as they watched it die. Mack climbed up onto his shoulder and shook his fist at the corpse. Bianca wasn't hurt and appeared to be barely shaken by the attack. His admiration for her grew.

"There's probably more of them," she said grimly. "They tend to roam in packs." It just proved that nowhere was safe in this area. Texas was littered with clones and droids. There were rumors that humans had begun to rebuild in some of the other states. Few managed to travel far enough to witness this for themselves. The vast desert killed most of them. Anyone who survived rarely returned to report on what they'd found.

"What are our options?" Loki asked.

"We can't run," she said as she headed for the door. "They'll swarm over us within minutes. We need to find somewhere secure to wait until morning."

"Where would you suggest?" he asked doubtfully. The other buildings were infested, from the sounds he could hear echoing around them. It was only a matter of time before the creatures sniffed them out. Bianca glanced up at the broken machinery used for drilling, then looked back at him. "You've got to be kidding," he complained.

"Not even a little bit," she said and ran towards the rusted hulk. Mack leaped from Loki's shoulder and rapidly climbed to the top. He showed her where it was safe to climb and guided them to safety just as the clones arrived. Sniffing, they knew prey had been here, but they were too stupid to think to look up.

Perched precariously on the wide beam on the top of the rig, Bianca had to fight down a grin at Loki's obvious consternation of their location. "Comfortable?" she whispered.

"No," he whispered back. "I find the accommodations in this place to be appalling. I won't be recommending it to my friends." Not that he had any friends to speak of.

She snorted out a quiet laugh, then they fell silent as the clones went out to hunt. From their vantage point, they watched as the hulking gray creatures hunted down anything that moved. Their appetites were prodigious and they kept up their search all night.

An hour before the sun was about to rise, the creatures began to return to their lair. "Who do you think they were before they were converted?" Loki asked quietly as the final monster disappeared into the buildings.

"They were probably employees," she said. "They might have returned to this place after Reaverton was eradicated just because its familiar to them."

His expression was a mixture of anger and pity. The Viltarans had invaded an innocent planet and had either cloned, or killed the inhabitants. Now the survivors had to eke out an existence on a dead husk of a world. While he was glad the aliens were gone, he almost wished he could meet one and serve justice to the creature. While he'd always harbored thoughts of rule, it sickened him to see the conditions Bianca had lived in during her entire short life.

They waited for the first rays of light to appear before they began to climb down. They were roughly halfway to the ground when Mack chittered in warning. Bianca looked up to see him pointing behind them. She turned around to see a unit of twenty droids approaching. They must have hurried to catch up to them, then crept in as quietly as they could.

"I think we may have a problem," Loki said as several of the silver robots lifted their small weapons.

Instead of pointing their disintegrator guns upwards, they shot at the rig. Bianca didn't even have time to curse before it began to fall. Metal squealed in protest at moving after decades of inactivity. The droids had weakened the base, leaving nothing to hold it up.

Loki reached, grabbed hold of Bianca and wrapped his arms around her as they fell. He created a magic bubble that encased them both. Mack was clutching Bianca's shoulder, eyes wide with fright. They hit the ground and the bubble saved them from receiving broken bones.

Sprawled on top of Loki, Bianca pulled her daggers. They wouldn't be much use against machines, but they were all she had.

Loki glanced at her weapons, then smirked as he made the bubble disappear. "I think Lævateinn will be of far more use," he said as they climbed to their feet.

"You named your sword?" she asked incredulously.

"I wasn't the one who named her, she was a gift," he explained. "If you'll give me a moment, I will rid us of these pesky droids."

She stayed close behind him as he conjured up a wide shield that shimmered slightly. The robots tried to blast it with their weapons, but they weren't calibrated to destroy magic. Darts full of yellow liquid splattered uselessly against the barrier as Loki strode towards them.

With no one left to maintain them, the metal men were beginning to break down. Their movements were slow and clumsy and he dodged them easily. He shielded Bianca and himself from harm as he swung his sword. The blade was magical and sheared through their arms, legs and necks without obstruction.

Within a few minutes, the unit had been wiped out. Scarlet eyes blinking rapidly, the final remaining droid made a buzzing sound of dismay as Loki lifted his boot. Its severed arms lay several feet away and its fingers twitched helplessly as he brought his heel down on the machine's face. Its eyes went dark, signaling its demise. "Well, that takes care of them," he said in satisfaction and let his shield drop.

Bianca's grin died when a lone robot stepped out from behind a clump of boulders. It raised its square weapon full of yellow darts and she knew they were both doomed. In desperation, she reached deep inside herself and sent a blast of power at the boulders. To her amazement, they formed into a crude body. The robot turned its head as the boulders began to move. It screeched in alarm when her minion lifted an arm and pounded the machine into the ground.

Loki stared at the squashed droid in astonishment, then turned just as Bianca lost consciousness. Without her magic to animate them, the boulders fell apart. He caught her and lowered her to the ground. Mack gently patted her on the cheek. He made small keening noises to see her so drained.

"She'll be all right," Loki said and hoped he wasn't lying. "She just needs rest." She'd told him it took a lot out of her to animate something big. Apparently, forging several boulders into a golem had pushed her over the edge.

Chapter Fifteen

Bianca wasn't out for long, but she was disoriented when she woke and realized Loki was carrying her. She looked up to tell him to put her down and sniggered. He'd wrapped the jeans around his head again and it looked even worse this time.

"Quite the fashion statement, no?" he said with an eyebrow quirked.

"I'm sure it'll catch on quickly," she replied huskily. He put her down and she realized he'd pulled the makeshift sleeves on her arms and had attempted to cover her head as well. She removed the denim from her head, shaped it into a hat, then donned it again.

"You make that look so easy," he complained and flicked one of the dangling pants legs with his fingers. Mack was riding on his shoulder and made a noise that sounded suspiciously like a giggle. "You think you could do better?" Loki challenged the monkey.

Screwing up his little face in concentration, Mack accepted the dare. He stood up and plucked the jeans into his hands. With a few deft movements, he made a far more usable hat and plopped it back onto Loki's head.

Rolling his eyes upwards, Loki had to concede that at least it wasn't as likely to fall off now. "Thank you," he said dryly. Mack bowed in response and wrapped his tail around the Asgardian's neck again.

Still chuckling, Bianca looked around to see the derelict oil rig was several miles behind them. "Where are we heading?" she asked.

Loki waved his hand at the arid wasteland. "In that direction," he replied.

Shading her eyes with a hand, she couldn't see anything. "Can you see something I can't?"

"I can just make out another oil rig. It will probably take us a couple of days to reach it." She nodded, too weary to comment. He waited for a few minutes before he spoke again. "Have you ever animated several different objects at once before?"

Bianca still felt woozy from using so much magic. It took her a moment to remember what she'd done. "I didn't think of the boulders as being separate. It was just one big pile of rocks to me."

"You forged them into a golem."

"What's a golem?"

"A creature made by magic that usually consists of rock, clay, metal and other substances."

"I panicked," she said, lifting a shoulder wearily. "I didn't really know what I was doing. I threw my magic at it, hoping it would stop the droid before it could shoot us."

"Well, I'd say it was a success," he said in admiration. "Your magic may be far stronger than you realize."

"I don't feel particularly strong right now," she said with a wan smile. "Thanks for carrying me, by the way. I hope I wasn't too heavy for you."

"Please," he said in mock insult. "You barely weigh anything."

"I guess a god like you could carry me all day," she retorted.

"I'd be happy to," he said silkily, reminding her of how he'd spoken to her in her dream. "But my services come with a price."

"What price?" she asked warily.

"One night in my bed."

"No thanks," she said dryly. "I'll walk."

"You mean one night isn't enough?" he asked in false surprise. "All right, you can have two nights." She laughed despite herself, but Mack crossed his arms and glared at Loki. "Easy," he said as the monkey's tail tightened around his throat. "I'm just jesting."

"That's what you get for teasing me when Mack is hitching a ride with you," Bianca said smugly.

"I'll try to remember that in the future," Loki said and tapped Mack's tail. The toy reluctantly eased his grip, but he chittered warningly.

They trudged through the increasing heat, stopping to cut hunks off cacti so they had something to chew on. The moisture helped hydrate them even though it tasted horrible. Without it, they wouldn't have made it this far. The dried coyote meat also helped to sustain them.

Loki had never been in such a desolate place, but he was startled to find he still wasn't having a completely horrible time. Something had shifted inside him and he wasn't sure exactly what it was, or when it had happened. He'd harbored dissatisfaction at his lot in life for centuries, but his jealousy of Thor and bitterness towards Odin seemed to have become less important. Maybe when his life wasn't in such dire peril, his usual annoyances and gripes would return. There was no point stewing about his ill treatment by his kin when he didn't even know if he would ever be able to leave this dismal world.

Seeing Loki's introspective frown, Bianca wished she had words of comfort for him. Apart from her, there was nothing magical on this world. She couldn't imagine they would find any means for him to return to his own dimension.

When they finally reached the abandoned oil field, they searched the buildings carefully this time. They were empty of clones, so they chose bunks and crashed. Mack watched over them as they slept.

Bianca couldn't remember any of her dreams when she finally woke. Loki had risen before her and had searched the other buildings more thoroughly. He sat at the small table with an ancient map spread out in front of him.

Yawning, Bianca sat across from him. "Find anything interesting?" she asked.

He flicked her a glance, then returned to his perusal. "We are roughly in the middle of nowhere," he said and pointed at a red spot he was fairly certain indicated their location. The map detailed all of the oil fields in Texas. It also showed the major cities. Reaverton was a short distance away, compared to the other places. It was another set of marks that had caught his attention. They couldn't keep travelling through the desert. The sun would eventually kill them. Traveling at night would be just as dangerous. The plan he had in mind was risky, but at least they wouldn't burn to death.

"What are you thinking?" Bianca asked. His expression was intent and focused.

He pointed at the black tracks that ran from Reaverton to the nearest large city. "According to this map, there is an underground rail system." It might not exist in every reality, but it did in this one.

She stared at him as if he was crazy. "There's bound to be clones hiding in the tunnels," she pointed out.

"They seem to sleep during the day and only go out at night to hunt. If we're careful, we should be able to make our way to Danely without being burned too badly."

"What do you think you'll find there?" she asked. "It'll be exactly like Reaverton; empty of people and crawling with droids and clones."

Sighing at her logic, he straightened up and stroked Mack's head. The monkey might not be a real animal, but he closed his eyes in enjoyment anyway. "We can't stay here," he replied. "We need food and water and I'd kill for a bath." Her face flamed red, instantly arousing his curiosity. "From the looks of it, you're also longing to feel water sliding over your naked skin."

She looked everywhere but at him, willing her cheeks to return to their normal color. "I've never had a bath," she said. "I've never had enough water to waste it like that." The natural springs in the caves she'd lived in had been far too shallow to submerge herself in.

"I promise you, one day you will have a real bath," he said solemnly. "I will personally bathe you if you like." His gaze slid from her face down to her chest and he leered at her suggestively.

"That won't be necessary," she said, crossing her arms over her chest grumpily. She could almost feel the weight of his hands against her again. Her dreams had never been so vivid before he'd arrived on her world.

"Let me know if you change your mind," he said with a wink, then returned to the map. "There appears to be a train station a few miles from here. It couldn't hurt to check it out."

Knowing he wasn't going to be dissuaded from his plan, Bianca sighed and stood. "Fine. Let's enter the train tunnel of death. I'm sure nothing bad can possibly happen to us."

"That's the spirit!" Loki said in a jolly tone. He carefully folded the map and placed it in the backpack. He hoisted it over his shoulder so Bianca wouldn't have to carry it, then plonked his makeshift hat on his head. He'd checked outside before Bianca had woken to see that it would soon be midday. There would be plenty of time for them to reach the station and see whether it was safe for them to use the train tunnels.

Chapter Sixteen

Now that Loki had a purpose, Bianca had to struggle to keep up with him. He finally realized she was lagging behind and slowed his pace to match hers. "Are you sure you don't want me to carry you?" he asked.

Seeing his sly grin, she made a face. "I'm not willing to pay the price it would cost me."

"Is the thought of spending the night in my bed really so terrible?"

Unable to tell whether he was being serious or not, she scowled. "The last time I was naked with a man, he betrayed me." Loki's jealousy instantly returned with a vengeance. "I'm not about to let anyone have that kind of power over me again," she added.

"Who could I possibly betray you to?" he asked in a logical tone. "From what I've seen so far, I'm your only friend in this world."

Mack poked the Asgardian's chiseled cheekbone in indignation and Bianca laughed. "You've insulted Mack. He was my friend long before you dropped into my life."

"He can't offer you the same type of comfort I can," Loki said smoothly and with a knowing smile.

"I don't need comfort," she retorted. "I was doing just fine before you turned up and ruined everything."

A bit hurt by that truth, he looked away. "You must wish you'd never met me."

Sensing his pain, she tried to make light of the situation. "I wouldn't say that. You gave Mack a boost so he doesn't need to use my magic to sustain him anymore."

"Wonderful," Loki said sarcastically. "My legacy on this world is that I have permanently animated a plush toy."

"At least you didn't invade us and kill, or enslave everyone," Bianca said bitterly. "The Viltarans sure as hell left a lasting legacy behind that I wouldn't wish on anyone."

"If I had the opportunity, I probably would have invaded Earth," Loki said in all honesty. "Not this version, obviously," he added with his upper lip curled in distaste.

"Why?" Bianca asked curiously. "What is the appeal in subjugating people?"

"Power is a heady experience," he told her. "Having the might to decide the fate of an entire world would be quite unlike anything I've experienced before."

She didn't have megalomaniacal tendencies and couldn't fathom why it would appeal to anyone. "I guess you have to be a god to want that sort of power."

"Not at all," he responded. "The Viltarans aren't gods, yet they seek supremacy over other species. There have been humans who have sought to rule lands other than their own." There had probably been many more since he'd last been to Midgard hundreds of years ago.

"I guess," she said, still unconvinced. "If you're the God of Mischief, do you think you'd really enjoy controlling an entire world? Wouldn't it be kind of boring after you'd enslaved everyone?"

"Probably," he conceded. "But quelling their resistance and bending them to my will would have been fun."

He said it wistfully and she couldn't tell if he was joking or not. "I hope you're not planning on trying to bend me to your will," she said darkly. She didn't like the tone of this conversation.

He looked at her for a long moment before smirking. "While bending you has great appeal, breaking you does not. I would much prefer you succumb to my dark charms willingly."

"Don't hold your breath," she said tartly, which made him chuckle in delight. He was just perverse enough to enjoy their strange banter.

The only indication they had that they were drawing near the train station was a single surviving concrete column. It had once been part of a building that had fallen down long ago. A set of metal train tracks that were badly eroded and were half covered in dirt led them to the entrance of the underground tunnel.

Bianca stared at the dark passageway in trepidation. It looked like the mouth of a huge beast. She didn't want to enter the darkness, but Loki was determined to use it as a method of travel. Her secret hopes that the tunnel might have collapsed were in vain. It had been well made and the sturdy concrete, metal and wood structure still held after all this time.

"Shall we?" Loki said politely, gesturing towards the tracks. He touched his sword and it began to glow softly. It gave off just enough light for them to see where they were going, but hopefully not enough to awaken any clones that might be hiding inside.

More than wide enough for them to walk side by side, the tunnel ran in a straight line. Every now and then, doors branched off into rooms. They didn't bother to try any of them. Neither of them were curious enough to see what lay behind the barriers.

From the scattered remains of bones, this was indeed a lair for clones. They finally encountered a small nest of them after they'd travelled a couple of miles. Loki doused the light from his sword and Bianca reached out to him in panic. He took her small hand and she held his fingers tightly. He leaned down to speak to her and she flinched when his hair brushed against her cheek. "They appear to be soundly asleep," he whispered. "I think we should try to sneak past them."

"I can't see anything," she said just as quietly. If she went blundering around, she would no doubt wake them up.

"I guess this means I'll have to carry you."

She could hear the smile in his voice and scowled. "You can keep going. I'm heading back."

"Oh, no you don't," he said and swung her into his arms.

"I am *not* spending the night in your bed!" she said in a furious whisper, trying to extricate herself from his grip. He was much stronger than she was and he held her easily.

"Since this is my idea, I'll give you a free pass," he said. "Now shush. Don't say a word until I tell you it's clear." He turned his head to see Mack shivering on his shoulder in fear. "That goes for you, too," he added.

Clapping his hands over his mouth, the monkey nodded obediently. He clutched Loki's neck with his tail, trying not to grip him too hard. He could see just as well in the dark as he could in daylight. Bianca was the only one who was blind.

Tense and breathing as quietly as she could, Bianca huddled against Loki as he made his way deeper into the tunnel. She almost let out a scream when Mack patted her arm in comfort. Loki made a small sound of amusement. Instead of sneaking, he strolled along as if he didn't have a care in the world.

It was easy to tell when they reached the nest of clones. Their stench gave them away. It was a combination of unwashed flesh and rotting meat from the bones that lay around them.

Keeping a careful eye on the monsters, Loki wended his way through them. Each one was identical, although some appeared to be females. These clones had short, fuzzy hair rather than being bald. Like the others, their ears were long and curled at the tips.

Some of them stirred as he walked past, sensing prey was near. He didn't pause and they soon settled back to their slumber. He waited until they were out of sight and hearing before he put Bianca down. His sword began to glow and she took a deep, shaky breath. "See?" he said smugly. "I told you using the tunnel would be a good idea."

"Let's just hope we can find somewhere safe to hide from them before the sun goes down," she retorted. The passageways had been designed to carry goods from the oil fields to the main cities and were dotted throughout the state. There would be many entrances and exits, which meant there were bound to be more nests of clones. Something told her this journey wasn't going to be as easy as Loki assumed.

Chapter Seventeen

It was hard to tell what time it was in the train tunnel. Neither Bianca, nor Loki had a watch. They only knew nightfall was upon them when they heard footsteps shuffling towards them. They'd passed an exit to a station a couple of miles back and there was nowhere for them to hide.

Acting swiftly, Loki grabbed hold of Bianca and doused the light on his sword. He raced back down the tunnel with his companion in his arms. Reaching the first doorway, he turned the handle. It opened with a rusty squeal and he ducked inside. The clones heard the noise and roared. He used his magic to lock the door, wincing as the sound of their rage echoed around the small space.

Completely blind, Bianca clutched his neck. Her breaths were coming hard and fast. Her breasts were pressed against his chest and he would have given anything to feel her naked skin against him. He was jolted out of his thoughts of lust as the nest of clones arrived. Luckily, they didn't hesitate at the doorway. They raced past, heading for the nearest exit.

Howls came from somewhere above, but they were from coyotes rather than clones. Roaring in glee and hunger, the gray monsters went on the chase.

Bianca sagged against Loki when she realized they were safe. "You can put me down now," she said shakily.

He didn't want to, but he obeyed her anyway. If he kept her in his arms any longer, he might do something stupid like try to kiss her. This wasn't the time, or the place to make his move.

Bianca relaxed slightly when Loki's sword began to glow again. She hated being in the dark and not knowing what was around her. Tran Li was the only man she'd ever trusted, but a year of living alone had given her self-reliance. She was used to taking care of herself and she didn't like having to rely on a virtual stranger.

Peering around, Loki found nothing of interest in the room. Rusty machine parts, tools and empty oil canisters were the only contents. "We should keep going," he said. "I want to cover as much distance as we can before we rest."

Bianca wasn't about to argue with him. She was tired, but she could walk for a few more miles before she would need to crash. Frankly, she was surprised the pampered Asgardian had managed to keep up with her for so long. Maybe he wasn't quite as spoiled as she'd assumed.

Keeping to a pace his much shorter companion could match, Loki continued along the tracks. He'd kept count of how many stations they'd passed so he would have some idea of how much further they had to go. When exhaustion made his steps drag, he guided Bianca towards the next door they came to. There was still a few hours before dawn, but they both needed to rest.

This door was locked and the handle had rusted shut. He used a burst of magic to unlock it and break it open, then another surge to lock it again. This room was mostly empty, so they chose a spot in the middle and sank down. Their water was running dangerously low, so they took small sips while eating dried coyote meat.

Loki waited for Bianca to curl up on her side and fall asleep before he doused the light. While she wasn't afraid of the dark, she clearly wasn't comfortable being in the lightless tunnel. He couldn't leave the sword glowing for fear the clones would see it when they returned from their hunt.

"You'll wake us if anything approaches?" Loki asked Mack. The monkey nodded and turned to face the door. Loki lay down facing Bianca. Her face stayed in his mind when he fell asleep.

In his dream, he was on another version of Earth that had also been invaded by Viltarans. Clones and silver droids hunted fleeing, screaming humans. He saw an alien that had to be eleven feet tall striding through a dark street. Black hair hung to his waist in stringy clumps. Like the clones, his skin was gray and his eyes were scarlet. His face was hideous and his teeth were almost as thick as tusks.

Bianca suddenly appeared on the street like magic. Standing beneath a streetlight, she turned in confusion. Instead of her usual black and brown leather outfit, she wore a tight-fitting green dress that emphasized her breasts. Seeing him, she held her hand out beseechingly. The gigantic alien raced towards her and Loki opened his mouth to shout a warning. Nothing came out and he was frozen in place as the monster punched his hand through Bianca's stomach. Blood and entrails poured out of her as the alien faded away.

"No!" he shouted and sat up. Grief and despair washed through him. He conjured up a light to check to see if Bianca was okay.

Bianca started awake at Loki's shout and reached for her daggers. He looked troubled and surprised her by placing his hand on her stomach. "What are you doing?" she asked.

"It was just a dream," he said in evident relief. "It seemed so real."

"What did you dream about?" she asked. Whatever it had been, it had shaken him to the core.

It was already fading and he frowned, trying to recapture it. "I can't remember," he said. "It was a nightmare, I guess." He smiled sheepishly, then turned to Mack. "Have the clones returned yet?" Mack nodded and held up one tiny finger. "An hour ago?" Loki interpreted and received another nod.

"That should be long enough for them to have fallen asleep by now," Bianca said. "We should head to the surface and grab some more cactus to chew on."

"Oh, joy," Loki said with a grimace. "I was so hoping you would say that."

"If we're lucky, I might be able to catch some more food as well," she added and he brightened.

"Why didn't you say so? Let's get going."

Straightening her shirt, Bianca looked down at her stomach, but couldn't see anything wrong with it. Had Loki been dreaming about her? If so, something bad must have happened. She was surprised that her pain had affected him enough to make him shout like that.

Trudging to the exit, they found bloody coyote bones strewn about on the surface. Giving them a wide berth, they headed for a clump of cacti. Bianca sliced off a couple of branches. She did her best to scrape the spikes off, then carefully placed them in the backpack. Loki insisted on carrying the pack as they both chewed on the horrible, but necessary plant. "Why don't we walk above ground to the next station?" he said around a mouthful of the awful substance.

Bianca sent him a grateful look. "You don't mind?" It was early enough that it wasn't hot yet. The next station would probably only be a few miles away.

"The fresh air will do us both good," he said. Even he was beginning to feel claustrophobic about being in the tunnels.

Bianca kept her eye out for food during their trek. She was rewarded by movement after an hour or so. Jogging towards the wriggling creature, she drew a dagger and threw it. It hit the mark exactly where she'd been aiming and she picked up the now headless rattlesnake in triumph.

"Ah, a snake," Loki said. "What's next on the menu? Vulture?" He could already see one gliding high above them. He frowned when he saw ruffled feathers in its right wing.

"Rattlesnakes don't taste that bad," she said defensively. "I hear they're a lot like chicken." Chickens were almost mythical creatures now, along with most animals. Almost every lifeform had been wiped out by the Viltaran gas. It was a miracle anything had survived.

With a heavy sigh, Loki watched Bianca butcher the snake. When it was skinless, he conjured up fire and cooked it thoroughly. She cut off a piece and offered it to him. He took it gingerly and tried it. "It's not as bad as coyote meat," he said after chewing and swallowing. "Much better than cactus." He was pretty sure this was the same type of meat they'd been eating before she'd killed the coyote.

Smirking, Bianca ate some of the snake as they continued their trek. "I'll make a native out of you yet," she said when she swallowed it down.

"Ugh," he said with a shudder. "I sincerely hope not. Earthlings are such pitiful creatures."

"One of us pitiful creatures knocked you out with a rock," she reminded him dryly.

He slanted her a dour look. "I assure you, that won't happen again."

"Uh, huh," she said to humor him. "A big, bad god like you would never let someone get the jump on him twice."

"Exactly," he said in satisfaction. "I am glad you are finally admitting my superiority."

Snorting, she pointed at the remains of the station. "Come on, your Lordship, the tunnel beckons."

They'd learned the clones tended to nest a couple of miles away from the entrances, so he made his sword glow as they descended into darkness. So far, their journey through the tunnels had been almost uneventful. He just hoped the trend would continue until they reached the next city.

Chapter Eighteen

Loki's plan to use the tunnels came to an abrupt end a couple of days later. Every now and then, they had to squeeze past an abandoned train. There was barely room for them to pass, but they managed it. This time, it wasn't a train that had stopped them.

"Well, this is inconvenient," Loki said as he studied the massive cave-in. The ceiling had collapsed, revealing the bright light of the sun above. "Now we know why we haven't passed any clone nests lately."

They'd passed an entrance a few miles back and they hadn't seen any clones during their trek. The gray monsters always kept their lairs a safe distance from the burning rays.

Bianca was secretly relieved to have a break from being in the tunnels again. Unlike the caves, these manmade passageways were small, cramped and unnatural. "We need to search for water anyway," she said. "We're almost completely out."

Loki nodded his agreement. He didn't relish walking through the boiling heat, but they needed to replenish their supplies. Bianca started climbing the rubble and he admired the view of her shapely legs and backside as she worked her way upwards.

Looking back over her shoulder, Bianca caught Loki staring at her and rolled her eyes. He chuckled in acknowledgement of being busted and started after her. They reached the top at the same time and clambered out into the open. They instantly began to sweat beneath the sun, but the moisture quickly evaporated. They donned their makeshift hats and protective gear until they were as ready as they could be for the grueling trek.

Delving into the backpack, Loki took the map out. His brows drew down when he realized they were still far from Danely. There were a few small towns along the way. One was only a few miles away, according to the ancient drawing. Lifting his head, he shielded his eyes and peered into the distance. Sure enough, he could just make out the ruins of a village. "I see a town ahead," he reported. "Perhaps we will find water there."

"That's doubtful," Bianca replied. "Even if we did, the droids would have poisoned it."

"You are such a pessimist," Loki scolded her. "Don't you ever try to think positively?"

She looked at him as if he'd gone crazy. "I haven't had a lot of experience with positivity," she said dryly. "My life hasn't exactly been a picnic, you know."

"Then it's about time things changed for the better," he said with a wink. "Now that I'm here, I'm sure your life will improve dramatically."

Astonished again by his overwhelming sense of self-importance, she shared a look with Mack. He was hitching a ride with her this time. The monkey made a rude sound. "I agree," Bianca said. "You're full of it," she said to Loki.

"Full of what?" he shot back. "Charm? Charisma? Stunning good looks?"

"Ugh, I can see why they kicked you off Ass Guard," she said drolly. "There probably wasn't enough room for everyone and your ego." His grin faded and she sensed she'd hurt his feelings. She reached out to touch his hand and he flicked her a glance. "I'm just joking," she said softly.

"You are more correct than you realize," he admitted. "I believed that I could rule Asgard better than Odin."

"Why?" she queried as they started towards the ruined town. "What qualifications do you have to be a ruler?"

He barked out a short laugh, then coughed. His throat was parched and his tongue was dry. "I've always believed I'm far more intelligent than most of my kin," he divulged. "In most cases, it's true." For once, his tone was introspective rather than arrogant.

"In hindsight, perhaps I need more experience before I attempt to take over my own world."

"Intelligence isn't enough to lead people," Bianca protested. "Unless you planned on being a tyrant." From his guilty look, she suspected her guess was correct. "You planned to rule with fear?" she asked.

"I would have ruled using whatever means were necessary," he corrected her. "If my kin had chosen to accept me, I wouldn't have had to resort to ruthless means. If they had rejected my rulership, then I would have stooped to other measures."

"Like what?"

"Such as allying myself with beings who could have given me the means to subjugate my people."

"You'd trust another species with that sort of power?"

He thought about it before replying. "Perhaps you are right. It would be very difficult to find allies who were willing to take on the Asgardian armies." Not to mention Odin. It would take someone very powerful to oust him from his throne.

They'd almost reached the derelict town when Mack surreptitiously poked Bianca's cheek to get her attention. He looked meaningfully at a clutch of boulders a few hundred yards away. Turning her head as casually as she could, she saw a figure crouched in the shadows. If Mack hadn't alerted her that they were being watched, she might not have discovered he was there.

"How many men are there?" Loki asked quietly as Bianca panned her gaze around.

"Three that I can make out," she replied. "There's probably more that I can't see."

"I thought there were few human survivors." It wasn't easy to pretend to be casual, but Loki kept his expression bland. Now that they'd been pointed out, he could see the men as well.

"There are probably caves somewhere near here," Bianca said. "They're the only places we have a chance of avoiding the droids." The survivors had fled to the desert after the invasion. They'd formed small societies in the caverns, eking out meager existences. "It's strange to see other people, but it isn't impossible for us to run into them every now and then."

"Hmm," he mused. He had the feeling there was nothing coincidental about this. He'd automatically hidden his sword upon leaving the tunnels. To the spies watching them, he would seem to be unarmed. They had no way of knowing he possessed magical abilities. But he suspected he wasn't the one they were interested in. Beautiful females had to be a rarity now. A woman like Bianca would be highly prized. Until they found out that she was a witch, of course. Once that became known, her popularity would take a drastic nosedive. "How do you want to deal with them?" he asked. If it was up to him, he'd fry them all before they could attack. But this wasn't his world and attacking first might not be the best option.

"We'll wait and see what their intentions are," she replied. Bianca was nervous and her hands kept trying to creep to her daggers. Mack was being very still, pretending to be a normal toy. It was crucial no one knew he was sentient or they'd figure out what she was. She didn't think they would have to wait long before the men would approach them. They would be in for a surprise if they chose to attack. Neither she, nor Loki were as harmless as they seemed.

Chapter Nineteen

It was late afternoon by now and the shadows were getting longer. They picked their way through shattered buildings, finding nothing of interest. Bianca followed her nose to the only water source. A busted pipe sluggishly oozed water. From the green fungus that had sprouted around the edge of the metal, it wasn't exactly healthy. One sniff was enough to warn her that the water wasn't drinkable.

Loki's hopeful expression fell when she shook her head. He desperately wanted to chug down an entire flask of water, but what he really craved was a bath. "What now?" he asked crankily. "Are we going to have to chew cactus during the entire journey?"

"If we have to," she replied evenly, then went on full alert when she heard stealthy footsteps approaching. Mack didn't protest as she stuffed him into the backpack. She drew her daggers and stood back to back with Loki as five men moved in to surround them.

Loki didn't draw any of the daggers from his hidden belt. He eyed the men warily as they examined them.

"You need water?" their leader said after an eternity of suspense.

"Yes," Bianca replied.

"You have something to trade?"

He reminded her of Craig, but his hair was dirty blond rather than red. Like her former leader, he had hard brown eyes. "We have coyote and rattlesnake meat," she told him. She'd hunted a few times and they had enough food to last them for a couple of weeks. She would gladly trade it all for some fresh water.

Considering her offer, he made a gesture for her to show him. She opened the backpack and grabbed a handful of the dried meat. He pursed his lips thoughtfully, then nodded. Hunting was scarce in these parts, thanks to the clones that infested the train tunnels. They had to travel miles away from their cave to find enough to feed their small group. "Follow us," he said and jerked his head.

Loki arched his brow and Bianca nodded. They needed water and this hunting party would lead them to some. There was no guarantee that they wouldn't just kill them and take their belongings after they reached their home, but she was prepared for treachery. In all honesty, she almost expected it.

The leader of the hunters ranged ahead, with his four men loosely surrounding Bianca and Loki. They weren't acting in a threatening manner, but their eyes were hooded and they were tense. Loki strolled along as if he owned the wastelands, smiling at Bianca whenever she looked at him. She wasn't as good at acting calm as he was. She darted suspicious glances at all five strangers. Her suspicion was to be expected when dealing with men she didn't know, so they wouldn't consider it to be unusual behavior.

Darkness fell as they finally reached a gorge that looked like it had been scooped out of the ground by a giant when the Earth had been young. Distant roars indicated the clones had woken and were hunting for prey. Faces paling, the hunters gave up on herding them and hurried ahead.

Bianca left several yards between herself and the final hunter as she followed them. Loki brought up the rear. She knew him well enough by now to trust him at her back. He could call on his magical sword and rend the men to pieces if they revealed themselves to be dangerous. She wasn't going to go down without a fight if they turned out to be raiders. Death would be preferable to being raped and tortured. Mack shifted in her backpack as if sensing her thoughts.

They took a narrow, winding path that had been made by running water long before the invasion had ruined Earth. The creek had dried up when the plants had mostly died and rain had almost become a thing of the past. When they reached the bottom of the gorge, the hunters wended their way through rocks and tumbleweeds towards a gigantic boulder. They disappeared behind it and light bloomed a few seconds later.

Bianca gripped her daggers, but she didn't pull them as she stepped around the boulder to see the mouth of a tunnel. Loki brushed against her back, peering over her head as the lead hunter waved for them to follow. He held a flaming torch in one hand and was impatient to get to safety.

It was comforting to be back inside a natural tunnel again as Bianca trailed after the five men. This passageway was far larger than her last home, or the previous one where she'd once lived. It opened into a gigantic cavern. Several family units were separated by low rock walls that had been painstakingly carried inside from the desert. They'd fashioned tents out of animal hides so they could have a semblance of privacy.

"This is hardly the sort of luxury I'm used to," Loki murmured. "But I guess it will have to do."

Bianca smirked slightly at his droll tone. She could see why he was called the God of Mischief. He was completely unable to remain serious for long.

A woman hurried forward to greet the hunters. She had short brown hair and was somewhere in her thirties. She'd probably been quite pretty when she'd been younger. Life was harsh and deep lines had been grooved into her face. In a few years, Bianca knew she would be exactly the same. Her beauty would fade and she would become just as worn down and tired as this woman was.

"Who are these people?" the woman asked fearfully. Strangers were rare and were feared.

"Just travelers looking to trade meat for water," he said soothingly and gave her a brief hug before turning to their guests. "I'm Kevin and this is my wife, Julie."

"I'm Bianca and this is Loki," Bianca replied.

"He's your husband?" one of the hunters asked.

"Not yet," Loki said before his small companion could reply. "We're engaged."

He grinned at Bianca winningly and she smiled reluctantly in return. It would probably be for the best if they pretended to be a couple. Maybe it would save her from being claimed by one of these strangers. It wasn't uncommon for battles to be fought over attractive females.

"You look exhausted," Julie noted. "Come and sit down. We have plenty of fresh water, but food is a bit scarce."

At the blatant hint, Bianca followed her to a fire and sat down. She reached into her backpack, careful to keep Mack hidden, and pulled out most of the meat she'd gathered. "I hope this will be enough to trade for water," she said.

Julie's eyes widened greedily at the supply. "It will do," she said and handed over a full flask. She gave Loki one as well and they both drank small sips so their stomachs wouldn't cramp in protest.

Loki stretched out his long legs and pulled Bianca against his side. She almost resisted him, then remembered he was supposed to be her fiancé. Leaning her head against his shoulder, she couldn't shake the feeling that they didn't belong here. If these people learned she was an exile, they would turn on them both.

"Where did you come from?" Julie asked as she handed out bowls of stew.

Bianca's mouth watered at the smell. She was delighted to see vegetables mixed in with the meat. Their diet of pure meat wasn't good for either of them. While they chewed the cactus plants for moisture, they spat the pulp out afterwards. Their stomachs couldn't digest the tough fibers very easily.

Loki took it upon himself to answer. He mimicked their accents perfectly, hiding the fact that he wasn't from this world. "We lived in a cavern near Reaverton," he said.

"Why did you leave?" Kevin asked. He'd taken a seat beside his wife and she handed him a bowl of food.

"Bianca was originally meant to marry someone else," Loki said. She kept her face bland as he spun his lies. "We fell in love and were cast out for our disobedience."

Julie nodded wisely and smiled at her husband. "Love can make us do crazy things," she said.

Kevin grinned and leaned over to kiss her on the temple. "That it can," he agreed.

It was a good performance, but Bianca had a feeling their happiness and hospitality was just an act. Loki stroked a hand down her arm, but she felt his tenseness. A hint of steel lurked behind his smile. He also suspected they were being played.

Finishing their meals, they followed Julie through a tunnel to their water source. Underground springs could sometimes taste foul due to limestone deposits and other minerals. Theirs was slightly metallic, but it was drinkable. They filled their flasks and she gave them two spares to fill as well.

"This is very generous of you," Bianca said as she knelt to fill the second flask. She tried hard to keep the suspicion out of her tone.

"We lost a hunting party a while back," Julie said sadly. "We have spares now."

"What happened to them?" Loki asked. He waited for Bianca to finish before he filled his flasks. By an unspoken rule, one of them was always on guard. They worked well together without needing to discuss their strategy in detail.

"Clones," she said in a clipped tone and crossed her arms tightly. "The hunters strayed too far away from our cavern and were caught out in the open. The critters tore them apart and ate them. We found their remains a few days later and scavenged what we could. Those creatures might have been people once, but they're worse than animals now." She shivered and her eyes were haunted.

"I'm sorry for your loss," Loki said and received strange looks from Bianca and Julie. Clearly, death was so common here that consoling the survivors wasn't the norm. He had a lot to learn about this version of Earth. Luckily, he had Bianca to guide him and hopefully prevent him from making too many mistakes.

Chapter Twenty

"I'm sure you'd both like to bathe," Julie said when they were finished filling their flasks. Bianca's head shot up and Loki had to grin at her eager expression.

"That would be great," Bianca said. It had been far too long since she'd had a decent wash. She had grit in some highly uncomfortable places.

"I'll show you to the pool we use to bathe in," their hostess offered and picked up the torch. She lit their way to another small cavern that had a shallow pool of water. It had a faint milky cast, which indicated it wasn't drinkable. "Don't swallow it," she warned them as she crossed to a stack of threadbare material that passed for towels.

"We won't," Bianca promised. The water in her cave had been fresh, but several pools in the main cavern she'd been cast out from had been similar to this.

Julie lit a torch that was attached to the wall by a metal bracket, then left them to bathe in privacy.

"You go first," Loki offered.

Her hands went to the buckles on her shirt and she realized he was still staring at her. "You're not going to be a very effective lookout if you stare at me the whole time," she pointed out.

With a heavy sigh, Loki turned his back. He was very tempted to sneak a peek at her as she stripped down and used one of the makeshift towels to clean herself. Crossing his arms, he gripped his biceps tightly and forced himself to keep watch. He was already hopelessly in lust with Bianca. If he saw her in all her naked glory, he wouldn't be able to think about anything else except bedding her.

Bianca didn't trust Loki and kept stealing glances at him over her shoulder. He stoically kept his gaze averted, but she could tell it cost him by his stiff posture. She sniggered quietly to herself as she used the homemade soap to wash her hair and body. The pool wasn't deep enough to immerse herself in, but she knelt on the towel and dunked her hair in to wash the soap out.

Finally clean and feeling a lot fresher, she dried herself and donned her clothing again. They desperately needed to be washed, but she didn't have anything else to wear right now. "I'm done," she said to Loki. He turned his head and his gaze travelled from her dripping hair down to her feet and back up again. His blue eyes were almost blazing with suppressed desire. She almost took a step towards him, then gave herself a mental shake. Nothing good could come of it if she gave in to the strange feelings he evoked within her.

Loki sensed Bianca's inner struggle and grinned inwardly. She was slowly coming around as she learned to trust him. Hopefully, she would soon realize that he wanted nothing more than to give her pleasure. Until then, he would have to behave himself, but it would be hard.

Speaking of hard, his body had reacted to the sounds of her splashing around in the water. His mind had conjured up an image to go along with the noises. Her eyes dropped to the all-too telling bulge in his trousers. She smirked as she stepped aside and took up his spot to keep watch. He didn't mind that she knew the effect she had on him. Seducing her wouldn't be easy. If she knew how much he wanted her, at least she would be prepared for it when he eventually made his move.

Bianca studiously watched the mouth of the tunnel as Loki stripped down. He made a sound of contentment as he splashed water on himself. Despite her resolve, she glanced over her shoulder. He knelt beside the pool, giving her a perfect view of his leanly muscled shoulders, back and butt. Heat flared in her face and she quickly looked away again. It had been a long time since she'd seen a naked man. Then again,

Sean had just been a boy. Loki was a grown adult and the sight of his nude perfection stirred an unfamiliar longing inside her.

Whistling beneath his breath, Loki soaped his body and hair, aware of the occasional peeks Bianca took over her shoulder. The fact that she found it hard not to stare was telling. It proved that she was attracted to him, which gave him a far greater chance of winning her to his bed.

In the back of his mind, he knew he should be focused on getting back to his own dimension. This wasn't a vacation that he'd willingly embarked on. He'd been banished and had ended up here by accident. There had to be a way back home, but right now he was more fixated on Bianca than with finding it. He'd never been this obsessed with a woman before, let alone a human one.

Seeing the frown on Loki's face when he joined her, Bianca didn't ask what was on his mind. His hair was as wet as hers and hung in clumps around his shoulders. She'd used her fingers to comb hers into a semblance of neatness. He did the same as she carried the torch to light their way back to the main cavern.

A few children had gathered into a group and were giggling over something. Seeing the strangers arrive, they went silent and looked suspiciously guilty. One of them was hiding something behind his back.

"I can't wait for you to have my baby," Loki said to Bianca as they neared the children. He caught a flash of red and blue fabric and knew what they were trying to hide. "I'm sure our children will cherish the toy monkey you've kept since you were young." He sent a sardonic look at the boy who had stolen Mack from her backpack.

Knowing he'd been busted, the boy shamefacedly stepped forward and handed the toy to the tall stranger. "We were just playing with it," he said defensively.

"You shouldn't take things that don't belong to you," Loki chided him as he took Mack from the thief. From their confused expressions, theft was a concept that was foreign to them. They were scavengers and everything they had was shared by everyone.

"It's okay," Bianca said with a smile at the chastened children. "No harm was done." That didn't mean she was going to let them take her friend again. Loki handed Mack to her and she cradled him in one arm like he was a baby. His body remained limp, but his eyes shifted to hers and he made a face. He apparently hadn't liked being pawed by the kids.

Julie picked up Bianca's backpack that had been discarded by the youngsters. "Sorry about that," she said with a stern glance at the offending children. "I'm sure you both want to get some rest. I'll show you to a spare tent on the other side of the cavern."

They followed her to the small, smelly dwelling. With a nod, she left them to get some sleep. Bianca opened the flap and crouched to enter. Loki had to kneel and shuffle forward on his hands and knees. As soon as the makeshift door closed, Mack leaped to his feet. He silently vented his indignation at his treatment by jumping up and down and shaking his fists in rage.

Loki shared an amused look with Bianca, then they both broke into quiet chuckles. "That was quite a tantrum," he said when Mack finally stopped his theatrics. "I hope you feel better now."

Disdaining to acknowledge Loki, Mack marched over to Bianca and climbed up to her shoulder. He snuggled against her neck, clearly glad to be able to move freely again.

Bianca lay down on some hides and found them to be soft and almost comfortable. Loki huffed out a sigh as he lay down beside her. Enough firelight filtered inside for her to be able to see his face that was only inches away from hers.

"You know, since we're engaged, perhaps we should play the part," he said with a mischievous grin.

"What are you talking about now?" she asked with a groan.

"Couples who are to be married usually engage in physical relations," he said seriously, but with a twinkle in his eye.

"I'm *not* having sex with you!" she hissed quietly.

He stroked a hand down her arm and smiled suggestively. "Our hosts will expect it of us, darling."

Slapping his hand away, she scooted as far away from him as she could get. "I don't care what they expect. It isn't going to happen." From the grunts and moans coming from other parts of the cave, no one would even notice if they did get naked together.

"We have to keep up appearances," Loki said and shifted closer. He was just teasing her, but seeing her reaction was worth it. Taking offense, Mack reached over and slapped him on the cheek. Gasping in outrage, he grabbed hold of the monkey. "Why you little…" Mack's tail whipped around his neck and they proceeded to try to throttle each other.

Bianca gaped at the pair who were locked in a furious battle. She sniggered and they both froze and turned to look at her. Collapsing onto her back, she laughed until tears gathered. When she finally regained control, Loki and Mack were staring at her coolly. "You can't choke a toy to death," she whispered to Loki solemnly. He scowled, which made her grin again. Mack put his hands on his hips and chittered angrily, taking offense at being called a toy.

"You're right," Loki said as if he understood him. "She needs to be punished."

Bianca barely had time to react before he rolled her onto her stomach and pinned her down with a hand on the middle of her back. He smacked her on the backside hard enough for it to sting. "Naughty girl," he admonished her, then rolled her onto her back again.

Breathless from being manhandled so easily, she opened her mouth to issue a tirade, but her angry words died when his mouth came down on hers. He kissed her thoroughly and expertly, making her insides squirm and heat flare deep inside her belly.

Pulling away, Loki saw a hint of blue in Bianca's hazel eyes. "I'll forgive you this time," he told her in a mock stern tone. "But don't make me punish you again." His gaze slid down her body and back up again. "I'll use something other than my hand to exact my revenge next time."

His tone was suggestive and his smile was playful. She didn't know how to deal with a whimsical god, so inserted a hand between their chests and pushed him away. "I'm going to sleep," she said sulkily, knowing it would be a long time coming. When it did, her dreams involved a naked Loki. As promised, he didn't use his hand to punish her.

Chapter Twenty-One

It would have been nice to linger in the cavern for a few days, but Bianca was already feeling restless. Loki also wanted to resume their journey. After breakfast, they stashed their full flasks in the backpack, making it obvious that they intended to leave.

Kevin ambled over when he saw them getting ready to leave. He'd kept his distance for the most part, leaving Julie to look after them. "There's something I want to show you before you go," he said. His tone was mysterious, as if he intended to divulge a little-known secret to them.

Exchanging a look with Loki, Bianca had a bad feeling that she couldn't quite hide. He arched a brow, leaving it up to her to make the decision. It would be rude to just leave, so she motioned for their host to lead the way.

"We've recently excavated a new tunnel," Kevin said as he grabbed a torch to light their way. Several hunters followed them, all carrying torches as well. The flames leaped, making their shadows frolic on the walls as they made their way through a narrow tunnel. "We found a chamber that defies description," he added mysteriously.

Intrigued, they followed him through the long, winding passage to a wide chamber. Stalagmites and stalactites adorned the high ceiling and perimeter of the floor. There wasn't anything particularly remarkable about them.

"Take a look at the center of the chamber," Kevin said and pointed at the floor that sloped upwards.

Bianca went first and walked up the slope to see a huge hole in the floor. Another chamber lay beneath this one. The ground was dirt and the walls were sheer rock. A single tunnel led deeper into the cavern. Turning to look at Kevin, she was startled to see he was right behind her. He grabbed her backpack, pulled it off her shoulder and shoved her hard. Pinwheeling her arms, she fell backwards into the hole.

Two hunters grasped hold of Loki and he was tossed in after her. The fall was a good thirty feet. Bianca landed on her back and the air was knocked out of her. Loki landed on his feet, caught his balance and raced over to her and dropped to his knees. Her face was pale and she was fighting to catch her breath. "Are you all right?" he asked. "Is anything broken?"

Luckily for her, the dirt was loose and deep enough to act as a cushion. She shook her head slightly and he helped her to sit up. Brushing dirt out of her hair, he ran his hand up and down her back and arms. She didn't flinch in pain and she seemed to be intact.

Glaring upwards at Kevin, Bianca saw him smirking down at them. "Why?" she croaked. It was all she could manage at the moment.

"One of Craig's people turned up a couple of days ago," Kevin replied. "He described you both and told us his leader would give us food, fresh vegetables and other supplies if we captured you if you came into our territory."

"We've been sold out for dried meat and carrots," Loki said in disgust. "Out of all the indignities I've suffered during my long life, this is at the top." He spoke too quietly for their captors to hear him.

"Craig and his hunters are camped a few hours from here and they're already on their way," Kevin informed them. "They've been tracking you ever since you fled from their cavern." He sneered down at Loki. "You shouldn't take what doesn't belong to you." His tone was mocking as he repeated the words he'd used to chastise the children.

Clearly, Craig had spun a story that was very close to the one Loki had come up with. Kevin and his people thought Bianca belonged to another hunter. They had no idea who she really was. That was probably the one thing that had saved them from being stabbed to death in their sleep.

Kevin didn't bother to post guards to keep watch over his prisoners. They couldn't climb the sheer walls. The only tunnel was blocked by a metal door after a hundred yards or so. They knew it was their only way out, but not even Loki's magic could open it. The metal was too heavy for Bianca to attempt to animate.

"We're stuck," Loki said, giving up on trying to pry the door open. He extinguished the small magical globe he'd created, plunging them into near darkness. A slight crack in the roof of the upper cavern allowed some light to filter inside as they made their way back to it.

"I could get us out of here if I had some rope," Bianca said. Mack was in the backpack and had probably been given to the children to play with again. She hoped he wouldn't do anything rash and give himself, and her, away.

"We will just have to bide our time and seize the opportunity to escape when it presents itself," Loki said with far more confidence than he felt. Taking a seat next to the curved wall, he patted the ground. Bianca sank down next to him and didn't protest when he put his arm around her shoulder. "Finally, we can have some time alone," he teased and received a tiny smile in response.

Judging by the rapidly dimming light, it was almost nightfall by the time Craig and his cronies arrived.

Hearing footsteps approaching, Bianca and Loki stood and looked upwards as flaming torches lit the chamber from above. Craig smirked when he saw them. Kevin and his men were nowhere to be seen. "I see you haven't managed to magic your way out of this trap, witch," he sneered. "I left two men behind to keep watch over Reaverton just in case you pulled a disappearing act. One of them followed you when he saw you sneaking out of the ruins. The other returned to warn me that you'd escaped justice again."

"I'll show you justice," Loki muttered as the last dying rays of sunlight disappeared.

Craig's smirk widened when guttural roars issued from behind the metal door that barred their exit. "You're not going to get away this time. You're going to hell where you belong."

Bianca turned at the metallic grating sound to see the door being drawn upwards. A hulking clone stood in the narrow passage. Scarlet eyes opened, blinked stupidly, then fixated on her. Letting out a bellow of hunger and rage, it ran towards her. Five more clones were on its heels.

Loki pulled Lævateinn and the monsters flinched from its shining brightness. Bianca drew her daggers and leaped forward to do battle with the creatures. She ducked and weaved, slicing and stabbing with precision. The first clone went down with punctured vitals and a slashed throat. Loki beheaded the beast that came for him, then spun around and impaled another one. From the corner of his eye, he saw Bianca engage another of the hulking creatures.

One of his adversaries grabbed hold of Loki and slammed him against the wall. It attempted to tear his arm off and he shouted in pain when his shoulder became dislocated. Putting his hand on the monster's head, he sent a jolt of pure magic into it. The creature wailed and smoke issued from its ears, nose and mouth. It collapsed, leaving a single clone behind.

Holding onto his injured arm, Loki watched as Bianca circled the final beast. Its crimson eyes were trained on her as she stalked it. Hers had turned dark brown with rage. She was beautiful in the heat of battle. His breath caught as she feinted to the right. The dull-witted clone fell for it and she darted to the left and got behind it. Her foot connected with the back of its knee and it went down. It let out squeals of agony as she rapidly stabbed it in the back multiple times.

Not yet content, Bianca rounded the clone and slashed her dagger across its throat. It fell onto its face and she tilted her head back to meet Craig's eyes, silently conveying that he would be next to fall to her blades. He'd tried to engineer her death several times now, but she wasn't going to give him the opportunity to do so again. One way or another, he was going to die.

Chapter Twenty-Two

Craig stared down at Bianca in hatred and fear. "I should have trusted my instincts and killed you at birth," he said, voice echoing around the chamber. His men shifted restlessly and were on the verge of running. Kevin had told them about the clones he'd trapped in the tunnel. They'd expected the monsters to tear the pair apart, but their plan had just fallen apart. "All of the Caldwell women are witches," he went on. "Whitney Caldwell's brat should have been strangled before she reached puberty. You're all cursed and it's because of your great-grandmother that our world was ruined."

Bianca flinched at the accusation that she couldn't deny. No man wanted to tie themselves to the Caldwell females and marry them, which was why she possessed her ancestor's surname. "You've been trying to kill me for years," she sneered. "Somehow, you keep failing."

"The Devil keeps his whores alive," he spat. "At least until they spawn a daughter to keep the Caldwell line alive. They don't tend to live long after that."

He said this with a hint of smugness that Loki found to be suspicious. He switched his gaze between Bianca and Craig, noting their similar hair color and features. "If you despise the Caldwells so much, why did you impregnate Bianca's mother?" he asked.

Craig's face paled and his men turned to stare at him in horror. "She bewitched me!" he said in desperation. "Just like Bianca bewitched Sean! He told me how she seduced him when she was barely thirteen. She got inside his head until he couldn't think of anything but her." His eyes went distant as he presumably remembered his secret relationship with Bianca's mother. "The same thing happened to me. I had no control over my body when I took that vile enchantress."

"What utter crap!" Bianca said in hot denial. "My mother wasn't a witch. She didn't have any power. None of the Caldwell women did, except for Whitney and now me. You probably raped my mother, just like someone did to *her* mother." Bianca's mother had told her herself and her mother had been abused. Even at six years old, she'd known what that meant. They lived in a cruel world where atrocities happened every day.

Craig went red, confirming her hunch. "She had it coming!" he hissed. "If I hadn't done it, someone else would have! You witches were made to seduce us with your beauty. We have to put you in your place and teach you your true lot in life!"

Rage swelled inside Bianca. Lifting her hand, she gestured at the bow he held. The string snapped and whipped out, scoring a deep cut in his left cheek. Blood sheeted down his face to drip from his jawline. "That's for what you did to my mother," she said in a low, vindictive voice. "Were you the one who killed her?"

"Yes," he snarled and used his sleeve to attempt to staunch the blood. "I found out she was pregnant again and I had to make sure she wouldn't create any more hell spawn like you."

Smiling almost serenely, Bianca concentrated on the bowstring that wavered in the air. "You're right," she said. "You should have killed me at birth." Learning she'd lost a brother or sister along with her mother had pushed her over the edge. She'd been six when Craig had killed her mother. This meant he'd been raping her for years after she'd been born. Before she could instruct the string to wrap around his throat and strangle him, arrows rained down from the hunters that circled them from above.

Loki pulled Bianca behind him and held his uninjured hand up. A shimmering shield encompassed them both as arrows descended. When the barrage was over, he decided he'd had enough of playing human.

The hunters stared down in shock at his display of magic. "Who *are* you?" Craig asked.

"I am a god, you bleating peasant!" Loki snarled. The men gasped in fright when the stranger's appearance changed suddenly. His green shirt and brown trousers became a black, gold and green leather suit. A long green cape appeared, along with a golden helmet with curved horns. "I am Loki, of Asgard and I do not come in peace," he intoned. He held his hand up again and sent a burst of fire upwards.

With shouts of alarm, the hunters scattered. Chuckling, Loki cut off the flames and dropped his hand. He turned to see Bianca staring at him with her mouth open. He flourished his cape and struck a pose. "Well?" he asked mischievously. "Do you like my outfit?"

"It's, uh, very impressive," she stammered. He'd said he was a master of illusion and now she saw his talents for herself. She reached out to touch the cape. It was even softer than it looked. "Is this real, or just my imagination?"

"It's real," he confirmed, then resumed his other guise of a simple shirt and trousers. "This is far more comfortable to wear in the desert."

His helmet disappeared as well and he became the man she'd slowly been getting used to. After that demonstration of power, she wasn't sure that she knew him at all. For all she knew, the personality he'd shown might also be a fabrication. The fragile trust that had built between them trembled on the edge of collapsing.

"We need to get out of here," Loki said, peering upwards. He cupped his left hand around his mouth. "Mack!" he shouted. "It's time to go!" His right arm was almost useless with his shoulder so badly dislocated.

As if he'd just been waiting for a signal, Mack popped his head over the lip of the hole. He examined them to make sure they were intact before throwing the backpack down to Bianca. She caught it and it was much heavier than she'd expected. She checked inside and saw it was full of food and water. The little scamp had pilfered back their stores, and more from the looks of it.

"He's an excellent thief," Loki said with a small grin. Sweat had popped out on his forehead, indicating that he was in pain.

Realizing his shoulder was hurt, Bianca put aside her concern that she didn't really know him at all. It would have to wait until they were gone from this place. "Is it broken, or just dislocated?" she asked.

"Just dislocated," he replied. "You'll have to put it back in for me."

"I'm not strong enough," she said and looked up at Mack. "Can you find me some rope?"

He scampered away and returned a short while later with a length of rope. He tossed it down and she caught it. At her command, the rope came to a semblance of life. Loki braced himself as best he could as the end wrapped around his wrist. With one hard yank, his shoulder popped back into place. Letting out a shaky breath, he gave her a small smile. "Thank you. I feel better already."

"You need a sling," Bianca said. At her direction, the rope slid beneath Loki's arm and around his opposite shoulder to secure it against his chest. The rest wrapped around his waist so it wouldn't drag on the ground.

"I wonder if we can escape through the tunnel?" Loki mused. The rope could probably drag them both out of the pit, but he didn't relish the idea of facing forty or so warriors and their bows and arrows.

Mack chittered, bobbing his head up and down in agreement. He leaped down and landed on Bianca's shoulder. He pointed at the tunnel, urging them to leave. The hunters had been scared away, but they would eventually regain their courage and attempt to attack them again.

Loki conjured up a globe and sent it ahead to light their way. The door that had blocked their way had slid into a slot in the ceiling. Only the bottom edge of it could be seen. The tunnel ran straight for a couple of hundred yards before they came to another door that had also slid upwards. "Did you open this?" Bianca asked. Mack nodded proudly. He'd followed Kevin to a mechanism that controlled the doors and had watched him operate it to let the clones in. The monsters had cleverly been lured between the two doors before being trapped. Kevin had used them as a tool to kill his enemies.

"He's a handy little fellow," Loki observed. "I'm glad my experiment to infuse him with my magic brought him to life."

Bianca frowned at the unmistakable self-satisfaction in his tone and remained silent. He'd boosted Mack's sentience and it seemed to be permanent, but she'd been the one to give the monkey a semblance of life in the first place. Her furry friend huddled against her neck, sensing her darkening mood.

Seeing the end of the tunnel ahead, Loki extinguished his globe. The hunters would have to be crazy to lay in wait for them now that night had fallen. As if in agreement, roars sounded from the clones that were roaming the wasteland in search of prey. Sneaking around them wasn't going to be easy, but they didn't have much choice. It would be certain death to remain near the caverns. They had to put as much distance between Craig, Kevin and the rest of the hunters as they could before their courage returned and they came after them.

Chapter Twenty-Three

Keeping to a fast walk that she could maintain for several hours, Bianca remained silent as they trekked through the night. The crescent moon was now able to give her enough light to navigate around obstacles without tripping over them or blundering into them.

Loki snuck frequent glances at Bianca, noting her distant expression. "Did you know Craig was your father?" He spoke quietly so his voice wouldn't carry to the hunting clones.

"No," she replied just as quietly. "I knew it was someone in the cavern, but my Mom never told me who had impregnated her."

"Did you really try to seduce Sean when you were thirteen?"

She shot him a glare at his almost prissy tone. "I didn't try to seduce anyone!" she said in self-defense. "He was the one who wanted to marry me when we turned fourteen." At his strange look, she explained their customs. "That's when children become adults on this world." It hadn't been her choice to pair up with Sean, but she wasn't in the mood to talk about it. "My magic kicked up another notch soon after my birthday and I couldn't hide it anymore."

"What do you mean, 'your magic kicked up another notch'?" he queried.

"I animated something for the first time just after I turned seven," she explained. "A girl was teasing me. She was taunting me and calling me a witch and a freak. I was mad and I wanted to hurt her. Something switched on inside my head and I reached out with my mind. I imagined her belt tightening around her, squeezing her to death and she started screaming and clawing at it." Her lips curled upwards in a humorless smile. "Luckily for her, my magic was weak back then and it barely left a bruise. She ran to her mother, telling her I'd tried to kill her. She was known as a liar and a bully, so no one believed her."

"Did something happen when you were fourteen that triggered another surge?" he asked.

"Yeah."

The stubborn set to her jaw indicated she wasn't going to tell him what had happened. Whatever it had been, it had gotten her exiled. "You seem to be growing stronger these past few weeks."

"I think my power has slowly been increasing for a few months," she admitted.

"You said you were twenty, correct?" he asked with a raised brow. She nodded in response. "When will you turn twenty-one?"

"In six months."

Loki hesitated for a moment before speaking. "It seems your magic gets a boost every seven years. I wonder how strong you will become after your next birthday?"

That was something she'd been wondering herself. Age seemed to have an impact on her magic. Whitney Caldwell had been a powerful witch, but her magic had been very different to Bianca's. Instead of being able to animate objects, she'd used elemental magic. It hadn't been enough to defeat the Viltarans and their unholy minions.

Bianca wondered why magic had manifested itself in her after so many decades. She flicked a look at Loki and knew what his response to that question would be. He believed she was destined to help him, which meant he thought of her as his lackey. He was easily the most arrogant being she'd ever met.

Feeling the weight of Bianca's stare on him, Loki turned to look at her, but she'd already turned away. He sensed that something had changed between them, but he wasn't sure what it was. Maybe seeing his full battle regalia had awed her and she now realized how powerful he really was. He preened a little, wishing he could wear his true clothing more often. Unfortunately, it just wasn't practical in this harsh environment.

Mack had been so still and quiet that Bianca had almost forgotten he was perched on her shoulder. She was reminded of his presence when he shivered and lifted a hand to point at something that she couldn't see.

"A clone is dead ahead," Loki whispered, moving closer to her side. "I'm going to try something." He cast an illusion that drastically changed their appearance.

Bianca let out a startled sound when she took on the form of an eight-foot clone with bulging muscles and short, fuzzy hair. She and Loki looked just like the monsters they'd killed in the chamber. He nudged her in the side and they loped forward. The clone saw them and howled a greeting. Loki howled back, mimicking the guttural sound perfectly. Satisfied that they were from its nest, the clone raced off to continue its hunt.

"I'm glad that worked," Loki said as they slowed to a walk again. His shoulder was throbbing in pain and jogging hadn't helped it much. He dropped the illusion, but was ready to resume it at a moment's notice.

"You're very good at pretending to be something you're not," Bianca said in a flat tone.

"So are you," he shot back, wounded by her suspicion. "You pretended to be human while hiding what you really were from everyone who knew you."

Turning to look up at him, her lips were pressed into a thin line. "What am I if I'm not human?" she asked. He remained silent, so she answered for him. "The Devil's whore? The final offspring of a line of evil witches?"

"The Devil isn't real," he scoffed. "If you were a whore, you would have allowed me to bed you by now. You are not a monster, Bianca, despite what the people you grew up with have told you." He sent her a chiding look. "You are better than them and they know it. That is why they revile you. You have powers that could crush them. Imagine what you will be able to do in six months when your power increases again." His eyes shone with an avid gleam.

"I don't want to crush anyone," she denied. "I just want to be left alone."

His expression turned knowing. "It is far too late for that, my dear. Craig, Kevin and their kin know that there are two magic users in this realm. Their fear of sorcery is so acute that they will spread the word that we exist. I am sure they are petrified that we might truly be a couple. They will fear that we could produce children who are even more powerful than we are."

That was a chilling thought and Bianca couldn't hold in a shudder. After her short and disastrous relationship with Sean, she'd given up on the idea of ever having children. The thought of having a child with someone like Loki was frightening. Their offspring would be hunted mercilessly and probably wouldn't survive their first year of life.

Chapter Twenty-Four

They encountered several more clones as they headed back towards the train tunnels. Loki disguised them each time and they remained unchallenged. He made note of the stations as they passed them. Each one had been built near an oil field. The hulking, rusty metal rigs dotted the horizon. They'd been growing more numerous as they headed eastward.

Dawn was maybe an hour away when Loki spied lights in the distance. He hadn't heard any roars from roaming clones recently and the area was eerily quiet. "I wonder what those lights are?" he said.

Bianca looked where he was staring, but her eyesight wasn't as good as his. "What lights?" she asked.

"It appears to be a settlement of some kind," he replied. "Should we investigate?"

"Why ask me?" she said in a surly tone. "You're the god."

Surprised by her snarky tone, he raised his brows. "Feeling testy, are we?" he said snidely.

"I'm just a lowly minion to you, aren't I?" Bianca demanded. "You think you're better than me." He remained silent, which was answer enough. "Just because you can use magic doesn't mean you're superior to everyone else," she said hotly.

"Actually, it does," he argued. "I am superior to humans in every way." It was a fact and no amount of argument could change that. "But we've already established that you aren't a lowly human," he said. He wasn't sure where her resentment was coming from. It just proved that women of all species were an enigma.

"But you don't think of me as your equal." She glared at him and he guiltily looked away, confirming her hunch. "Since you're so high and mighty, Loki of Ass Guard, I'm sure you'll do just fine out here in the wastelands on your own."

"You're really going to leave?" he said incredulously as she turned her back on him and walked away. Her sudden anger was unexpected and he had no idea what had set her off. "Where are you going to go, Bianca? No one on this planet wants you here. They'll hunt you down and eradicate you. Without me to hide you from the clones, you won't last a week!" He was shouting by now, uncaring if the clones in the nearby area heard him. Not that there seemed to be any.

Bianca stopped, turned and gave him a cold stare. "I've managed to survive for twenty years without your assistance, oh Great Lord and Master of the Entire Universe." Her sarcasm was thick enough to make him wince. "Out of the two of us, you're the one who won't last a week." She delved into her backpack and tossed two flasks of water at him. He caught the first one, but with only one good hand, he dropped the second one. "I'm sure you can catch your own food," she said coldly. "Use an illusion that you're a snake to get close enough to one to stab it in the back. I don't think you'll have to pretend too hard to pull that off."

He opened his mouth to retaliate, but she turned and trudged away. Mack lifted a hand and waved forlornly. He looked like a small child who'd witnessed his parents fighting for the first time.

"The nerve of that woman," Loki muttered and bent to pick up the fallen flask. He was bewildered by her sudden change of attitude towards him. He had no idea what he'd done to deserve this. Being called a snake had cut him to the quick. It was one of the insults his kin had used against him as he'd been growing up. He'd always pretended it hadn't bothered him, but it did. It hurt even more coming from someone he'd hoped to get naked with one day soon.

Steeling himself, he tucked the flasks beneath his injured arm and headed towards the lights that were blazing in the distance. It was the first true sign of civilization he'd seen so far. He was curious about the people who were brave enough to announce their presence so brazenly.

He trudged along, taking the occasional sip of water and chewing on cactus branches to keep his body hydrated. Darkness was encroaching again when he closed in on the small town. He could hear a loud machine chugging away and assumed it was powering the lights. The air was thick with fumes from whatever substance the machine ran on. A metal wall about thirty feet high had been scrounged from a nearby oil rig. A small door appeared to be the only entrance. Guards stood on platforms, keeping watch.

His arrival was noticed and seemed to create a bit of a stir. As he drew closer, he saw the guards were all female. Their hair had been cut in strange styles that almost made them seem masculine. Most were shaved, except for a strip down the middle. Others had their heads shaved on only one side. Tattoos decorated their scalps, arms and bits of flesh that he could see beneath their rough clothing.

Another head appeared above the doorway as he approached. This woman wasn't as hard in the face. Her Mohawk was blond and her tattoos stood out starkly against her pale skin. She stared down at him imperiously, then smirked. "Look at this," she drawled. "A man has come to call on us. Should we let him in, ladies?" She called this out and received hoots and jeers in response. "I think I'll take that for a 'yes'," she said with a grin that didn't reach her eyes.

Loki started to have a bad feeling about this town. It worsened when the door opened and ten women swarmed out to surround him. All carried spears, knives or bows with arrows drawn. They might as well have had the word 'reaver' tattooed on their foreheads. He'd never seen female raiders before, but that was exactly what they seemed to be.

"This is quite the welcome," Loki said charmingly. He used his real accent, hoping to be enough of a curiosity that they wouldn't just kill him outright. He didn't relish the idea of striking women down, but he would if he had to.

One of the women patted him down, but he hid his sword and daggers from her. She took his flasks and the rope and he winced when she jolted his shoulder. "Be gentle with me," he said with a grin. "I'm still recovering from an encounter with a clone."

Their blond leader appeared in the doorway and looked him up and down. Her eyes were light brown and assessing. He felt like a prized horse that had been taken to market and was about to be sold to the highest bidder. "I'm Silvia," she said. "What's your name?"

He had a feeling she didn't really care, but he answered her anyway. "Loki Laufeyson." He didn't bother to tell her his origins. They wouldn't have heard of Asgard anyway.

"Welcome to our town, Lucky," she said. "I'm sure you'll fit right in."

Her grin was toothy and he lost all desire to correct her mispronunciation of his name. He knew in his bones that these women would kill him. First, they would want to have some fun with him.

He smiled graciously and followed her through the doorway. They would soon learn that he wasn't the easy prey he appeared to be. They might have killed or cowed all other men they'd encountered, but he was a different beast entirely. Their blades and arrows would be no match for his magic.

His arrogant confidence began to wither as they made their way past small houses that were mostly made of metal. Men dressed in simple loincloths toiled away on the buildings, or tilled an extensive garden. They shot fearful looks at the women guarding them. Ugly red burns were scattered all over their bodies. These women had turned the tables and had become the more dominant gender. They seemed to be making their captives work at all hours of the night and day.

His captors guided him towards a building that rose a few feet above the others. Silvia climbed the short flight of metal stairs and imperiously gestured for him to follow. He climbed after her with his entourage of reavers at his back. The remnants of his bravado fled when he entered the house and saw what was in store for him. Before he could attempt to use his magic, something hard crashed into the back of his head. As he lost consciousness, he had a rueful thought that Bianca would laugh at him for letting himself be stricken down by a pitiful human again.

Chapter Twenty-Five

Bianca looked over her shoulder, expecting to see Loki watching her walk away. Instead, he was already striding towards the town that was too far away for her to see. Strangely hurt that he'd dismissed her so easily, she let out an inaudible huff and turned away again.

She set a fast pace that soon slowed when the sun became a burning weight. They'd left their makeshift hats behind in Kevin's cave. The harsh rays beat down on her, burning her scalp and arms where her gloves didn't cover them. Her anger fueled her and she silently fumed as she headed into the wastelands.

Two days later, she was exhausted from not sleeping well during the few hours she'd allowed herself to rest. She decided to take a short break from the heat. Seeing a clutch of boulders, she trudged over to them and sat down in the meager shade. It would be midday in an hour or so and the shade wouldn't last long. Sweat trickled down her brow and she wiped it away with her arm, almost dislodging Mack from her shoulder. He scampered down to her lap and stared up at her solemnly.

"What?" she said dourly. "Do you have something to say?"

He took that as an invitation to vent and let out a tirade of noise. None of it made any sense to her, but his gestures were clear enough. He thought she was an idiot for driving her only human friend away. Or maybe *Asgardian* friend was more accurate. Loki had made it very clear that he wasn't human.

"You heard him," she muttered sourly. "He thinks I'm beneath him because I'm not from his world." Mack rolled his eyes and put his hands on his hips. He tapped a foot impatiently, clearly expecting her to come to her senses. "He's probably dead by now anyway," she said. Strangely, the thought gave her an unwelcome pang. "The odds that the town he saw is full of nice, normal people are pretty low," she added. Anyone brazen enough to advertise their presence had to be dangerous.

Mack made a frightened sound and launched himself at her, hugging her neck tightly. "You're scared for him, aren't you?" she asked as she stoked his back. Mack nodded and huddled against her. "I'm sure he isn't really dead," she told him. "He's too clever to let himself be killed by lowly humans." Her attempt as humor fell flat and he glared up at her. "You're not going to give up until I check to see whether he's okay, are you?" He shook his head and his expression turned stubborn.

A nagging sense of guilt had been pawing at her conscience, urging her to go after Loki. It was getting harder and harder to ignore. She sensed he was in danger, but it wasn't her job to babysit him. She'd already saved his life. Why did she have to follow him around and keep him from doing something stupid?

Scowling at the thoughts that swirled through her mind, she heaved a sigh. No matter how mad she was with him for being so arrogant and superior, his parting words had been true. No one wanted her on this world and she had nowhere to go. He intended to find a way off this planet and she was starting to think that was a good idea. There were apparently other dimensions of Earth. If she could help him find a way to get home, maybe she could find a place where she wouldn't be considered a freak.

"Fine," she said in capitulation. "I'll go after Loki and rescue him from whatever disaster he's no doubt gotten himself into." Mack clapped his hands in glee and jumped up and down on her lap. She laughed, then coughed at how dry her throat was.

The sun did its best to punish her as she trekked back the way she'd come. Her pace picked up when night fell and she was exhausted by morning. She reached the abandoned train station and decided to sleep beneath the ground for a while. She hadn't heard any roars from clones and the place seemed to be devoid of them.

Taking the stairs downwards, she didn't stray far from the entrance. Without Loki's magic, she couldn't see a thing down here. Unlike him, she couldn't conjure up a light. Using her backpack for a pillow, she lay down on her side, facing the stairs. Enough light shone down for her to see a few feet in all directions.

Mack scampered off into the darkness. He returned a short while later holding something in his hands. His eyes were round with fear as he handed the object over. It was an arm bone, but it was much larger than normal. "You think this came from a clone?" she asked. He nodded, clutching his hands together. "Something killed it?" He nodded again and held up his fingers to indicate there had been six of them. "They killed the entire nest?" she asked and he nodded again.

No wonder she hadn't heard the clones. Someone had eradicated them. Her concern for Loki increased with this knowledge. Her intuition told her that the people who lived in the mysterious town were responsible. In his sheer arrogance, Loki had probably marched right up to it, declared his name and expected them to bow to his magnificence.

Trusting Mack to watch over her, she fell asleep with Loki on her mind and he featured in her dreams. He sat on a strange chair that allowed him to recline backwards. His legs were so long that his feet hung over the edge of the plush chair. His expression was pensive. Turning his head, he saw her and desire darkened his eyes.

She looked down to see she was wearing something that wrapped around her. It was black, soft and felt silky against her skin. Feeling as though someone else was controlling her, she crossed the room, climbed onto the chair and straddled his legs. He was just as shocked as she was when she leaned in to kiss him.

His hands went to her shoulders and she thought he was going to stop her. Then his mouth was on hers and he kissed her. His tongue slid between her lips and she opened her mouth to him. Sean's fumbling attempts had been pitiful compared to Loki's skill. His hands went to the sash holding her robe shut and it parted beneath them. Sucking in a breath, she nuzzled his jaw as his hands cupped her flesh reverently.

"You have perfect breasts," he whispered in her ear. "It is as if they were made for me to fondle."

Leaning into him, she brushed her lips on his neck and he shivered. "Do you like it when I kiss you there?" she asked breathily.

"Yes," was his hoarse response. "But I imagine I would enjoy your lips on any part of my body."

She moaned when he gently squeezed her breasts, then bent to take a nipple into his mouth. She'd never felt desire like this before and hadn't even known it was possible to want someone so much. Digging her hands into his long hair, she felt something tighten deep inside as he sucked deeply on her breast. Instinct made her rock her hips forward so their groins met and it was Loki's turn to groan. She rubbed against his hardness and he lifted his head from her breast and kissed her deeply.

"Finally," a female voice said in satisfaction, startling Bianca into pulling away. She turned her head to see a tall, skinny blond woman with a Mohawk standing behind her. Naked, she was almost completely covered in tattoos. "It's about time you got it up, Lucky."

Shocked into waking up, Bianca's breasts ached as if they still felt Loki's hands and mouth on them. Rolling onto her back, she looked up the stairs to see darkness was about to fall. "That was a very strange dream," she said to Mack. He looked at her, then motioned towards the stairs, urging her to get a move-on. "All right, I'm going," she complained and hauled herself to her feet. Loki probably needed to be rescued and somehow, she'd become the hero who would have to swoop in and save him.

Chapter Twenty-Six

Loki was lost in a dream about Bianca. She was naked and her breasts were just as perfect as he'd imagined them to be. Round and full, they fit into his large hands perfectly. He was so lost in the dream that he didn't realize the hands that were stroking him were real until a strange voice spoke. "It's about time you got it up, Lucky," Silvia said, then attempted to straddle him.

Waking up, he bucked his hips and twisted his body, dumping the leader of the reavers onto the floor beside the bed. His injured shoulder only protested a little at the movement. It was nearly healed even though his arms weren't in the most comfortable position.

Taking stock, he saw he was still naked and was still shackled to a rickety old bed. The springs sagged badly enough that his back was smarting. A mattress made of smelly old rags was far from comfortable. He'd been held captive for four days now and he'd resisted Silvia's attempts to seduce him admirably. The only reason he was still alive was because he hadn't succumbed to Silvia's dubious allure. She'd used her hands, mouth and body to attempt to get him to have sex with her and he'd refused to respond. One dream about Bianca had almost been his undoing.

"I'll kill you for that!" she snarled as she shot to her feet. She snatched up a rusty dagger from a rickety bedside table and held it to his throat.

"Go ahead," he said in a bored tone and tilted his head back to give her better access. "Death would be preferable to catching a disease from you."

Gasping in outrage, she slapped him hard enough to split his lip. Knowing she would do something she would regret if she stayed, she turned and stalked out.

Loki's desire rapidly faded and he looked around groggily. He saw the shadow of someone standing in the hallway next to the door. Silvia and her entourage had him under guard night and day. Unlike their other prisoners, he hadn't been branded by fire yet. His looks and strange accent were enough to pique Silvia's interest. He wasn't sure how much longer she would resist her urge to maim and kill him.

When he'd first stepped into this house, he'd seen torture implements laid out on rusty metal tables. Bloodstained shackles were attached to the walls. Several chairs also sported shackles that were stained with bodily fluids. The haunted and pitying looks from the few men he'd seen had become crystal clear. He'd been knocked out before he realized it and had woken up strapped to Silvia's bed.

The fog in his head made it hard to think. He tried to grasp hold of his magic again, but failed. His captor had no idea he was a magic user, but she kept him sedated by drugging his water anyway. "Where are you, Bianca?" he whispered in despair.

He wished he knew what he'd done to drive her away. He would take it back and try to make her realize how much he depended on her. He'd let his pride rule him and he'd let her walk away instead of asking her to stay. Now he was trapped and he would soon become a victim of rape. He uttered a short laugh at the absurdity of someone of his power being in this position. His only hope was for a fragile young woman to rescue him from his predicament.

As the hours passed, he tried again and again to grasp hold of his magic and failed each time. One of Silvia's henchwomen entered with a glass of water and plate of dried meat. She eyed his naked body with an insolent smirk. They probably believed he was pleasuring Silvia every time she entered the bedroom. He wasn't about to jeopardize his life by setting her straight. "Thirsty?" she asked with a grin. Several of her teeth were missing and the rest were yellow. Some were showing signs of rot. She was barely in her twenties, but she might as well have been elderly. Like her mistress, she had a short strip of hair running down the middle of her head. Hers was brown rather than blond.

"Not really," he lied. His concentration was beginning to return. In another hour or so, he would probably be able to extricate himself from this horrible trap.

"Too bad," she said snidely and plonked the food and water down on a nightstand. "The boss says you have to be watered every six hours."

He tried to yank his head away when she grasped hold of his hair and lifted his head, but she was stronger than she looked. She poured water into his mouth, then held his jaw shut until he swallowed. His head began to swim a few minutes later and he pliantly allowed her to feed him. "Silvia told me to cut back on the drugs," she told him as she fed him strips of meat. "She says you aren't performing as well as she'd hoped." She leered at him and grabbed hold of his manhood. When he didn't respond to her rough strokes, she frowned. "Looks like I'll have to cut back on the drugs even further," she murmured. This time, she only gave him half of the water, but she fed him all of the meat.

He smiled at her dreamily when she was done, pretending to be more deeply affected by the sedative than he really was. Right on cue, Silvia entered shortly after her henchwoman left. Loki pretended to be asleep as she stripped down and her mouth closed over him. She did her best to make him erect, but he felt nothing but revulsion for her and he didn't respond.

Finally giving up after trying for over half an hour, Silvia pulled her clothes back on and stomped away. She was stopped just outside the door and he listened in to their conversation.

"You need to see this," her main henchwoman said. "We have a new arrival and she's demanding to see you."

"This should be good," Silvia replied with an audible sneer. "I feel like beating the crap out of someone right now."

"Did I put too much of the drug into your new pet's water again?"

"Yeah," Silvia said. Her frustration came through loud and clear. "He might as well be dead from the waist down."

"Maybe he prefers men. You should try dressing as a guy. That might turn him on."

"Don't be an idiot," Silvia said as she strode away. "He was moaning the name, Bianca, in his sleep earlier. As far as I know, that's a girl's name."

Their voices faded and Loki breathed a sigh of relief. With luck, the haziness would fade from his mind soon and he would be able to break himself free. When he managed to escape from here, he vowed to track Bianca down and apologize for whatever he'd done to annoy her. Clearly, he couldn't survive in this harsh world without her.

Chapter Twenty-Seven

Heading in the same direction Loki had gone a few days ago, Bianca followed his occasional footprint. The ground was too hard and arid to record every step he took, but he'd left enough signs for her to follow. This was how Craig's hunters had managed to follow them from Reaverton. She'd been trained not to leave a trail, but Loki was new to this world and he still wasn't used to the dangers. She would have to take better care to make sure he didn't leave scuff marks again.

Finally seeing lights blazing in the distance, Bianca increased her pace. Mack shifted restlessly on her shoulder and she wished her eyesight was as good as his. She slowed down when she drew close to the walled town so the guards wouldn't see her. They were all female and looked like hardened hunters to her. It was strange not to see any men standing guard.

Walking around the perimeter of the settlement, every inch was being watched. There was only one visible entrance, although she was certain sections of the wall could be shifted at need. They had to get the large scraps of metal they scavenged into the place somehow.

Since it wasn't going to be possible for her to sneak in, she would have to talk her way inside. Loki's footprints had led her here, which meant he was somewhere inside. She was about to approach the gate when she heard voices speaking. Stopping just outside the range of the lights, she strained to listen in.

"Silvia's new toy is so gorgeous that I wish I could have a piece of him," a rough female voice said.

"You and me both," another woman responded with a harsh laugh. "I bet every woman in this place would kill for a chance to ride him. He's prettier than most of us are."

Indignation instantly rose inside Bianca. It withered before she could become angry that she'd trekked so far just to find out he was having a grand old time when the first woman spoke again. "He won't stay pretty for long," she predicted in a knowing tone. "Silvia will use him up and set him to working just like the others."

"If she doesn't kill him first," the second woman said, then laughed nastily. "I hear he isn't as willing as most men usually are to fulfill her needs."

Bianca's blood ran cold when she realized what was going on here. This was a town full of female reavers. They must have killed the clones in the area, probably waiting for daylight before sneaking into the tunnels and slaying them. This was a relative safe zone that would draw the occasional victim straight to them. They killed the men they didn't want and enslaved the rest.

"Loki has gotten himself into more trouble than I'd realized," Bianca whispered to Mack. He nodded solemnly in response. The question now was how she was going to get him out of this mess. If these women were the warriors they appeared to be, the only thing they would respect was might. Being only five-foot-two, she wasn't the least bit intimidating. Thanks to Tran Li, she was far from helpless. First, she had to get inside the walls. Then she would have to somehow free Loki from his apparent captivity.

Taking her backpack off, she held it open. "In you go," she said to Mack. He heaved a small sigh and crawled inside. She closed the flap, but didn't tie it so tightly that he couldn't escape if he needed to. Dawn was almost here and she would be spotted soon. It wouldn't be a good idea to look as if she'd been spying on the town, so she hiked a short distance away and waited.

When the first rays of light appeared, she trudged towards the gate. It wasn't hard to pretend to be weary. If they thought she was fatigued, she would have a better chance of pulling off her rudimentary plan.

The guard watching the gate went on full alert when she spotted the visitor. "What do you want?" she sneered.

Bianca looked up, keeping her expression blank. "I was separated from my boyfriend a few days ago when we were attacked by clones," she said. "I followed his footprints here."

"I don't know what you're talking about," the guard said, eyes darting to the side.

"You're a bad liar," Bianca said. "Go and get whoever is in charge of this place. I want Loki back and I'll challenge her to a fight if I have to."

The guard barked a harsh laugh. "That I'd love to see. Silvia will stomp you into mush, little girl." She turned and called out to someone, then exchanged a quiet conversation with them. "You're going to wish you never came here," the guard promised her with a wide grin.

"Believe me, I already do," Bianca murmured. Even if she did challenge their leader and defeated her in battle, it sounded like dozens of women were living here. She couldn't help but wonder why Loki hadn't used his magic to free himself. It occurred to her that he might actually be enjoying his captivity. That thought evaporated when the gate was yanked open and a tall, skinny blond woman with a Mohawk appeared in the opening. It was the woman from her dream and Bianca had to work to keep her expression blank.

Light brown eyes assessed her, then Silvia sneered in derision. "I hear you're looking for me."

"You have my boyfriend and I want him back."

"What makes you think he's here?" Silvia said, leaning against the doorjamb nonchalantly and studying her tattered fingernails.

"I heard your guards talking. His name is Loki, by the way, not Lucky."

Annoyed that the girl had spied on her town without her knowledge, Silvia looked the intruder up and down. "He's too much man for a little thing like you to handle. I think he'd be better off here with real women who can appreciate him." Her stare was as insulting as her tone.

Bianca had known it would come to this. "I challenge you to hand-to-hand combat," she said. "If I win, Loki and I get to walk away unharmed."

Silvia snorted out a laugh. "You are seriously deluded if you think you can beat me in a brawl," she said, then jerked her head at the gate. "Come on in, Princess. It's going to be fun to beat the crap out of you in front of your boyfriend." She said this with a jealous sneer she probably wasn't even aware of.

Following Silvia through the gate, Bianca noted the suspicious stares from the guards. They all wore stained, filthy clothing and were covered in tattoos.

Flat and hostile eyes followed her as she trailed after Silvia to the center of the small town. All of the buildings were made of metal that had been scrounged from the nearest oil field. A few men toiled away beneath the hard stares of the armed female guards. Her stomach churned at the unsightly burn marks that marred their flesh.

"Wait here," Silvia ordered her, then stalked towards a building that had been raised higher than the others.

Bianca took a sip of water as she waited, acting as if she wasn't worried about the upcoming fight. Women began to gather until a sizable crowd surrounded her.

"Make way," Silvia snarled as she descended the stairs.

Two of her henchwomen held Loki in their clutches. They were tall, yet he loomed over them. From the way he was blinking owlishly, he'd been drugged. Seeing Bianca, he smiled widely, making her heart lurch. "I knew you'd come for me, darling," he said as the crowd parted to let them through.

"You're my fiancé," Bianca said and hoped he wouldn't ruin the ruse that they were a couple. "Of course I came for you." His pleased grin faded when he was wrenched to a halt. He winced at a flare of pain in his injured shoulder.

"The intruder has challenged me to a fight for this man," Silvia shouted. "The winner gets to keep him. What punishment do you think the loser should get?"

"Death!" someone shouted and the chant was taken up by everyone.

Silvia motioned for them to quiet down and smiled nastily at the much shorter woman. "You heard them. It looks like I'm going to have to kill you."

"Not if I kill you first," Bianca shot back. She'd suspected their fight would end with one of them dying. Now she just had to make sure she didn't lose.

Chapter Twenty-Eight

Bianca dropped her backpack and drew her daggers. In return, Silvia took a machete from one of her guards. They circled each other, looking for openings. Training with Tran Li had been brutal at times and Bianca had suffered bruises and concussions as he'd tried to toughen her up. Despite all of her training, she'd never taken a human life before. Judging by Silvia's bloodthirsty grin, she was well acquainted with murder.

Silvia lunged forward and Bianca side-stepped, then sliced a shallow cut down the raider's arm. Snarling, Silvia spun around and attempted to punch her in the face. Bianca blocked the blow with the pommel of her dagger. Bone crunched and Silvia let out a hiss of pain. She wasn't used to fighting someone with martial arts skills. Her left hand was now useless and she only had her machete to rely on.

Ignoring the crowd who were shouting and jostling each other to get a better look, Bianca focused on her enemy. She knew she was far more skilled than her foe. She could easily slice her apart, but that would surely incite a riot among the women. Her goal was to take her opponent down without hurting her too badly. Maybe then, she and Loki could still be able to walk away unscathed.

Silvia feinted a wild swing, then tried to kick the intruder in the stomach. The smaller woman didn't fall for her ruse. She deflected the kick with a sweep of her arm, leaving a long cut on Silvia's leg.

Bianca could use her hands and feet just as effectively as her knives. She performed a brutal sidekick that broke a couple of ribs from the crunching sounds they made. Silvia gasped and went down on one knee. Bianca casually stepped behind her and delivered a precise blow to the back of her head with the pommel of a Sai. Knocked out cold, the leader of the raiders sprawled in the dirt.

Loki chuckled and attempted to applaud, but the henchwomen held him fast. "I knew you would be victorious, my love," he beamed, swaying on his feet from the drugs. "Let us leave this horrid place immediately and never return."

"You're not going anywhere," Silvia's second in command snarled. "Kill her!" she ordered the shocked mob.

Bianca had known deep down that they wouldn't be able to leave so easily. The women pulled their weapons and rushed her. Seeing a rope lying discarded on the ground, she brought it to life. It stood on one end and whipped out in a circle around her, knocking her opponents down.

"She's a witch!" someone shouted and panic broke out.

Most of the women scattered and ran for the exit. A few remained, intent on killing the magic user. Releasing Loki, the guards ran to help. Now free, he reached for his sword that he'd surreptitiously belted around his waist when he'd been cut free from the bed and had been ordered to dress. His head swam and his muscles didn't obey him. The weapon dropped from his grasp, hit the ground and became visible.

Silvia's main henchwoman spied the weapon. She strode over, bent down and tried to pick it up. The moment her fingers touched the sword, it blazed with silver light. A burst of electricity went through her and she jittered from the force of it before falling onto her side. Smoke issued from her mouth and her glazed eyes stared into nothingness.

"Serves you right," Loki slurred and picked the weapon up again. "That's what you get for drugging me and fondling my manhood without my permission."

Bianca was too busy using the sentient rope to keep her foes at bay to pay attention to what Loki was doing. She didn't want to kill any of the women, but they were making it hard for her. Male shouts of triumph came from behind her. She turned to see the prisoners fighting with their captors. A small flood of men emerged from the largest house. She saw a young woman with her head shaved only on the left side darting away with a determined, yet frightened look on her face.

The men joined the fight and Bianca let the rope drop before they realized she was a witch. She didn't want them to turn on her. Backing away from the brawl, she sidled around to Loki. He was having trouble staying upright and was waving his sword around dangerously. "Put that thing away before you hurt yourself," she said.

Staring down at her in affront, he tried to focus on her blurry face. "I assure you, despite my current state, I am quite capable of using my sword."

He leered and she rolled her eyes at his double meaning. "We need to get out of here while the women are distracted," she told him. "That's going to be hard enough without you tripping over and stabbing me in the back by accident."

"I see your point," he conceded and sheathed the weapon.

Mack appeared, dragging the backpack behind him. No one had noticed him in the melee. He scampered up to Bianca's shoulder when she bent to pick up the pack. They only had two flasks of water between them now, but she didn't have time to search for the ones that had been taken from Loki. She just wanted to get the hell out of this place.

Looking around, she saw the young woman who had apparently freed the prisoners waving at her from her hiding spot next to Silvia's house. From the desperation on her face, she was determined to speak to them. Curious despite herself, Bianca took Loki's arm and hurried towards the girl.

"Are you really a witch?" the girl said when they reached her. She was about eighteen and was probably pretty beneath the grime. A tattoo of a knife on her shaven scalp looked like it had been done fairly recently. Her hair was black and her eyes were almost as dark as her hair. Her flawless skin was a lovely olive color.

"Yes," Bianca replied. "But I don't want to hurt anyone. I just wanted to rescue Loki and leave in peace."

"These bitches don't understand the meaning of the word," the girl said bitterly. "They killed my family a few months ago and kidnapped me. They've been trying to brainwash me into becoming one of them."

"What's your name?"

"Ashley."

"I'm Bianca and he's Loki. If you can get us out of here, you can come with us." Loki frowned at her offer, but he didn't protest. Mack nodded eagerly and Ashley's eyes widened when she saw him moving.

Gulping in fright, she made her decision. "Wait here. I'll be back in a minute." She darted off and ran inside Silvia's house. She emerged a couple of minutes later carrying a heavy backpack. "This way," she said and headed to the back of the house. Stopping at the wall, she pulled a lever and a wide section of the wall between Silvia's house and the one next to it opened. "Hurry," she said. "I'll close it after you leave."

Bianca guided Loki through the opening so he didn't trip over his own feet. He was smiling happily as if there wasn't currently a slaughter going on behind them.

Ashley pulled the lever again and darted outside before the wall could descend and trap her in the town. She shouldered the backpack and looked at Bianca. "What now?" she asked.

"Now we run before anyone realizes we're gone." Holding onto Loki's hand, Bianca took off. Ashley huffed and puffed, but kept up with them. They ran for a few miles until she was sure they were out of sight before slowing down. She tried to let go of Loki's hand, but he entwined his fingers with hers and strolled along as if he didn't have a care in the world.

"They drugged him pretty good," Ashley noted as she tried to catch her breath. "Silvia normally treats her slaves like animals. He's lucky she didn't brand him like she did all the others."

Bianca looked up at Loki to find he was staring at her with a serious expression. "You saved me again," he said. He was sounding more with it now. Maybe the run had helped clear his head. "You're starting to make a habit of it after all."

"Yeah, well, we both know you would have been dead within a week without me," she grumbled. "Mack convinced me to go after you."

Loki grinned at the monkey. "It looks like I owe you as well."

Mack bobbed up and down, chattering noisily.

"What the hell is that thing?" Ashley asked. She knew it wasn't a real animal, but she'd never seen anything like it before.

"His name is Mack," Bianca replied. "He's a toy monkey that's become sentient."

"Right," Ashley said in a faint voice. "A toy monkey that's somehow alive. Makes perfect sense." She uttered a wild giggle that hinted of encroaching insanity. Then she took a deep breath and blew it out. "Do you have a destination in mind, or are we going to wander around the wastelands forever?"

"We're heading towards Danely," Loki said. "We should be halfway there by now." His head was becoming clearer by the minute as the drugged fog lifted. Danely wasn't their ultimate destination. It would just be one step along the way. He was more determined than ever to leave this hellish world after his recent ordeal.

Glancing down at Bianca, his heart swelled with gratitude that she'd come for him. Her mysterious anger seemed to have drained away and she was back to her usual aloof self again. With Ashley now trotting along beside them, he couldn't voice the words that were roiling inside his head. He would prefer to speak to Bianca privately. God only knew when he would have that opportunity now.

Chapter Twenty-Nine

Ashley had loaded her backpack with food and water, but she'd packed another item that came in useful when the heat of the midday sun became unbearable. "Can we stop for a couple of hours?" she panted. Sweat dripped down her face, but it was too hot for her clothes to remain damp for long. The sun evaporated the moisture too rapidly.

Bianca judged the girl's condition and realized she needed a break. She looked around for shade, but the sun was directly overhead by now. There was nowhere for them to find shelter.

"I stole a tent," Ashley said and knelt. She rummaged around in her backpack and brought out a folded sheet of canvas. She opened it to reveal a bunch of short metal rods. They were designed to be fitted together to prop the tent up. It was only meant for two people, but they managed to squeeze inside. They left the tent open, but there was no wind to stir the air. It was stiflingly hot, but at least they were out of the sun.

Loki had to sit directly in the middle due to his height. "Tell us about Silvia and her merry band of murderous women," he said. His mind was completely clear and sharp again.

Ashley brought her knees up to her chest and wrapped her thin arms around them. "As you've probably guessed, they're reavers. The town was originally built by settlers a decade or so ago. They hunted down the clones in the area and intended to start up a trade between any nearby communities they could find."

"What happened to them?" Bianca asked when the girl paused.

"Silvia happened," Ashley said bitterly. "Rumor has it that she was attacked by raiders and was nearly killed. She got away and stumbled across the town. They took her in and nursed her back to health. In repayment, she murdered their leader with a knife and poisoned most of the men. She told the women that they could stay if they agreed to join her. She convinced them that men were evil and that they shouldn't have to be their whores just to survive."

"She was insane," Loki said in a clipped tone.

"Yeah," Ashley agreed. "They all knew she'd kill them if they refused, so they joined her. They learned how to fight and killed most people who came to the town. Silvia kept some of the men as slaves and forced us to have sex with them." Her expression reflected her disgust at what she'd had to endure. "She intended to breed more raiders, all female of course." She didn't have to spell out what happened to any male children that had been born.

Bianca's eyes flashed dark brown, giving away her rage. Loki caught her gaze and saw her anguish that she apparently felt for both him and Ashley. "Silvia was unsuccessful in her many attempts to rape me," he told her gravely. "My will was too strong for her to conquer."

Ashley snorted out a laugh. "There was a rumor that she couldn't make you sleep with her," she said with a snigger. "She was obsessed with having sex with you and nothing she could do worked."

Loki's smile didn't reach his eyes. "It almost worked," he whispered just loudly enough for Bianca to hear him. "I had a dream about you that had me quite…worked up."

A blush rose on Bianca's cheeks as she remembered the dream she'd had about him. Somehow, she'd dreamt about Silvia before she'd even met her. "Did it have a chair that let you lean backwards with your feet dangling over the ends?" she asked wryly.

Stunned, he stared at her strangely. "Yes, actually."

Her breath caught and she was just as surprised as he was. "I saw a woman standing behind us in the dream," she whispered. "It was Silvia." Realizing they were having a private conversation, Mack leaped over to Ashley's shoulder and chittered in her ear to distract her.

"How is this possible?" Loki asked with a frown.

"I don't know." They stared at each other, worried that they'd somehow managed to share the same dream.

A sly smile appeared on Loki's face. "I owe you for saving my life, or at least my virtue. I'm sure there are many ways in which I can repay you."

Flushing to her hairline, she knew exactly how he wanted to repay her. She cleared her throat, determined to ignore his endless flirting. "You can start by telling me what happened when that reaver touched your sword." She spoke in a normal volume, signaling that their private chat was over.

With a sigh, Loki tore his gaze away from her delectable breasts. The memory of that dream was going to haunt him. Especially now that he knew how passionate Bianca could be. She'd let her guard down in her dream, but when she was awake she erected a barrier between them. "I have warded Lævateinn so I am the only one who can touch her," he explained.

"You named your sword?" Ashley said with a slight smile. "And you think of it as female?" She'd been freaked out by the monkey when it had first leaped onto her shoulder, but he seemed harmless. His tail was wrapped loosely around her neck and he snuggled into her despite the overwhelming heat. He wasn't really alive, so maybe the temperature didn't bother him.

Loki pretended to be affronted by her incredulous tone. "Of course she's female. She's both beautiful and deadly, which is a combination that only females can pull off successfully." He patted the weapon he'd laid on the ground beside him. "I didn't name her, though. She was a gift."

"Who *are* you?" Ashley asked. "You don't look or sound like you come from here."

"He's from a planet called Ass Guard," Bianca said and Loki flicked her a dark look. "Excuse me, your Highness, I meant *As*gard," she said sarcastically. "It's in another dimension," she explained.

Ashley shook her head in confusion. "There are other dimensions?"

"There are an infinite number of realities," Loki told her. "I fell into this one while escaping from some unruly aliens."

"This just gets weirder and weirder," Ashley muttered. She'd wanted to escape from the reavers ever since she'd been kidnapped, but now she'd ended up with a witch and a being from a planet she'd never heard of.

"He's a magic user, too," Bianca said. Their new friend needed to know everything so she could decide whether she wanted to stay with them, or strike out on her own.

"I kind of figured that," Ashley said. She'd seen Silvia's right-hand woman die after touching the sword. He'd also said he'd warded it, which sounded witchy to her. Studying them both, they didn't seem to be all that different from normal people. "You don't look evil," she said. "I always thought witches were the Devil's spawn."

Loki chuckled dryly. "Hardly. The Devil doesn't exist. He's just a fabrication that humans invented to frighten their children into being good."

"You mean this isn't hell?" Ashley asked, waving a hand at the desolate view through the tent opening. "I thought we'd all been sent here to be punished for something."

"Don't you know the history of our planet?" Bianca asked.

Ashley lifted a shoulder and let it drop. "Not really. I know something bad happened because of a witch a long time ago. The people from my cavern didn't really talk about it much."

"Whitney Caldwell tried to save our world," Bianca said in defense of her long-dead ancestor. "She failed and the Viltarans won. They unleashed their droids and clones and wiped out most of mankind. Then they gassed the planet, killing most of the animals and plants."

"Who were the Viltarans? Some kind of aliens?"

"Yeah. When I was a little girl, my Mom told me they look a lot like the gray clones, only bigger and uglier." The picture she'd seen in the ancient newspaper in Reaverton had confirmed that.

"How could your Mom know that?" Ashley asked with a hint of suspicion.

"Because Whitney Caldwell was my great-grandmother," Bianca admitted. "The people in the cavern where I grew up knew the real history of our world better than most."

Instead of running and screaming, Ashley's brown crinkled thoughtfully. "So, your great-grandmother was a witch and you are, too?"

"Yep."

"Does that mean you're going to try to save our world now?"

"What? No!" Bianca didn't want that burden. She noted Loki's sardonic look. They'd already had this conversation, but he'd come to the conclusion that she existed just to serve him.

"Why not?" Ashley pressed. "You have magic. Maybe you can use it to kill the clones and droids."

"Even if I could, it's far too late for this world," Bianca said with a hint of desperation. "It's already beyond saving."

"You can't possibly know that," Loki said. "You've only seen a small portion of Texas. For all you know, other parts of the world might be recovering from the gas."

She sent him a fulminating glare and received an innocent smile in return. "I'm not a hero," she said tightly. "I'm just trying to survive."

"You saved my life more than once," he pointed out.

"You saved me, too," Ashley added.

Bianca stubbornly shook her head. She didn't want to save this already dead world. She just wanted to find somewhere safe to spend the rest of her lonely life in peace.

Chapter Thirty

When the heat of the day abated a bit, they packed up the tent and continued on towards Danely. Ashley struggled beneath the weight of the pack and Loki took it from her without a word. She smiled wanly in thanks as he shouldered the burden.

As they walked, he mused about his circumstances. He'd banded together with the most nefarious and hated woman on the planet. Not many knew who or what Bianca was yet. She was basically his equivalent on this world when it came to notoriety. Word was bound to spread that another Caldwell witch lived. Once it did, they would be hunted by everyone.

He was used to having servants at his beck and call, but this world was very different from his. He was the one hauling their gear like a beast of burden. A strange sense of camaraderie had sprung up between the three of them already. They were all outcasts and they had a better chance of survival if they stuck together.

Bianca was scanning the horizon, looking for trouble. Mack rode on her shoulder, swiveling his head to check behind them frequently. With him as a lookout, no one was going to be able to sneak up on them.

Loki spoke, startling Bianca after a silence that had lasted for some time. "Have you tested the limits of your magic?" he asked.

"Tested it how?" She hadn't exactly had anyone to teach her about what she could and couldn't do.

"Such as determining what sort of objects can you animate?"

"Of course. I can only animate small things mostly. Nothing that is already alive."

"You mean you can't take over a person and make them do stuff?" Ashley asked.

"Nope. It doesn't work on animals, plants or people." She'd tried to force bullies to leave her alone when she'd been a kid, but it hadn't worked.

"What is the largest thing you've animated?" Loki queried.

"The boulders I used to smack down the droid."

Ashley almost missed a step. "You can animate rocks?"

"Sure," Bianca replied and pointed at a stone around the size of her head. "Watch this." At her command, the small boulder began to roll along beside them.

"What else can you make it do?" Ashley asked. She was a bit creeped out by the display, but she was also fascinated.

"Nothing, really. It's not exactly something that's easy to manipulate. Rope is a lot easier because it's flexible and it can stand up and move around."

"Have you tried to animate your daggers?" Loki asked.

"No. It never occurred to me to try."

"Try it now," he suggested.

Still walking, she drew one of her daggers and infused it with magic. It moved in her hand, indicating it was temporarily sentient. "Now what?" she asked.

"Try throwing it and see if it'll come back to you."

She raised a skeptical eyebrow. "How could it possibly come back to me? If I throw it, it'll just fly in one direction." He continued to stare at her patiently and she huffed out a sigh. "Fine. I'll give it a try."

Aiming at a cactus that stood a few yards away, she hurled the dagger at it and ordered it to return to her. Just as she'd expected, it kept flying towards the plant. It attempted to follow her command, but all it could do was flip over until the tip was pointed at her. The pommel hit the cactus and it fell to the ground.

Ashley's upper lip curled in fear when the weapon began to flip end over end as it made its way back to its owner. She couldn't help her superstitious dread of anything magical. It had been ingrained into her since birth. "That is so creepy," she said with a shiver.

Bianca bent to retrieve the weapon, but Loki moved before she could sheath it. He grabbed hold of Ashley and pressed a dagger that he pulled from nowhere against her neck. The girl gasped in fright and held onto his arm, trying uselessly to pull it away. "What are you willing to do to save your new friend, witch?" he said. His tone and expression were menacing. It was like an evil version of him had taken over his body.

"What are you doing?" Bianca asked. "Have you gone insane?"

"Are you just going to watch her die?" he asked her harshly. He lifted Ashley up so she shielded his face and body from her. His dagger pricked her skin and she let out a small shriek.

Calmness came over Bianca. She didn't know what the hell was wrong with Loki, but she wasn't about to stand by and let him kill Ashley. Whipping her hand up, she threw the dagger. She didn't want to hit Ashley, so she aimed for a spot just beside Loki's head. Concentrating hard, she willed the dagger to curve at the last moment. The pommel crashed into his temple hard enough to draw blood.

Loki's vision doubled and he dropped Ashley. His legs wobbled and he was suddenly sitting on the ground.

Mack pointed at him and let out a shriek of laughter. Doubling over, he fell off Bianca's shoulder and landed on the ground with a thump. He giggled wildly, legs kicking spasmodically.

"Was that a test?" Bianca asked suspiciously. She stood with her hands on her hips, alternating her glare between Loki and Mack.

"Of course," Loki replied. He lifted a shaky hand and touched the bleeding wound. Wincing, he pulled a handkerchief from out of thin air and dabbed the cut. "I thought you might perform better if you had enough incentive."

"Thanks a lot," Ashley grumbled. "A bit of warning would have been nice."

"That would have defeated the purpose of the test," Loki said dryly. "I needed your reaction to be real, or it wouldn't have spurred Bianca to react."

Shaking her head in exasperation, Bianca withdrew her magic from the dagger and strode over to retrieve it. She slid it back into the sheath and knelt beside Loki. "Let me see," she said and brushed his hand away. The cut wasn't bad and the bleeding had already stopped. "You'll be fine," she told him. "But don't do that again, or the pointy end might hit you next time."

"Let me see your daggers for a moment," he said and held his hands out. An idea had seized him and he didn't stop to think about the consequences.

Still kneeling beside him, she drew them both and held them out. Instead of taking them from her, he wrapped his hands around hers. He sent a surge of power into the daggers, inadvertently pulling her magic out of her at the same time. They came alive beneath her hands as she animated them, then everything went dark as her consciousness was drawn somewhere else.

Standing in utter darkness, she could see Loki standing beside her. Before she could ask what had just happened, two figures appeared in the gloom. She saw herself and a hulking gray alien that was more than twice her height. He pulled his arm back, then punched his hand through her stomach. Loki took her hand and they watched as another version of him appeared. He knelt beside her twin and it was clear he was distraught by her impending death. The scene faced, leaving them in darkness again.

"What was that?" Bianca asked. "Was it real?"

"I don't know," Loki replied. He was just as disturbed as she was. "This is the second time I've seen this," he told her, recalling a nightmare he'd had. "It seems so real."

"It can't be," she said. "Unless we're seeing other versions of ourselves in another dimension."

Loki grasped at the idea. "That must be it," he agreed. "But why are we seeing it?"

"Maybe it's a warning of some kind," she mused. The darkness began to fade and they snapped back to reality.

"What happened?" Ashley asked when her new friends stirred and pulled apart. Mack was huddled on her shoulder, staring at them in worry. "You both froze up for a few seconds." She'd tried to speak to them, but they'd ignored her as if she didn't exist.

"I think we had a vision," Bianca replied. "We saw different versions of ourselves from another dimension."

"What were they doing? Did you speak to them?"

"Something attacked me and I think I was dying," Bianca responded as she slipped her daggers back into their sheaths.

"It was clear that we knew each other," Loki added. He stood and offered Bianca his hand. She took it and he drew her to her feet. "We don't know what the vision meant," he added.

"I think it was a warning, but I don't know about what," Bianca said.

"What killed the other version of you?" Ashley queried. This sort of mystical stuff was beyond her comprehension.

"I think it was a Viltaran," Loki told her. "It was around eleven feet tall and had the same sort of gray skin and general appearance as the clones."

"Except it was way uglier," Bianca said. "It had scarlet eyes, fangs, long ears that curled at the tops and matted black hair that hung to its waist." It was an exact copy of the image she'd seen in the newspaper.

"Ugh, it sounds even more horrible than the clones," Ashley said as they continued their trek. "I'm glad they all left our planet."

"So am I," Bianca agreed. It had been disturbing to see herself with a gigantic hole in her stomach. The other version of Loki had been enraged and full of despair when he'd crashed to his knees beside her twin. She couldn't shake the feeling that they'd been more than just friends. From the speculative glances her version of Loki kept sending her, he suspected the same thing.

Chapter Thirty-One

They walked until the sun fell below the horizon, then took a short break. According to Loki's estimation, they were currently halfway between two train stations. They couldn't hear any clones hunting nearby, so he risked a fire. He'd killed a rattlesnake just before they'd made camp and he roasted it over the flames.

Turning to the two girls, his grin faded when he saw a gray monster rushing at them from the darkness. Mack shrieked in alarm as the clone swung its meaty fist at Ashley. Bianca pushed her new friend aside and pulled her daggers. She'd forgotten that she and Loki had infused them with magic. The memory came rushing back when they came alive in her hands and she was dragged forward as they lunged at the monster.

More clones appeared until they were surrounded by six of the creatures. From the corner of his eye, Loki saw Bianca struggling to control her weapons. He'd also forgotten that they'd used their magic on them. Just like what had happened to Mack, he'd done something to change them. His magic combined with Bianca's seemed to have a potent effect.

He drew Lævateinn and the clones flinched from the blazing silver blade. Ashley huddled next to the fire. Her arms were shielding her head as her friends battled the creatures.

Bianca grunted in pain when a gigantic fist caught her in the ribs. Several bones snapped and the daggers suddenly stopped fighting her as though they suddenly became aware of her peril. Instead of trying to attack the clones on their own, they waited for her to command them.

Slicing at the offending clone, the blade didn't just score a cut on its wrist, it severed the beast's hand. The hulking thing stared down at the bright yellow blood that spurted from its stump, then looked at her stupidly. Bianca did her best to ignore the pain in her ribs and slashed out again. Her blade sliced across its throat, almost cutting its head off.

Their combined magic hadn't just brought the blades to a semblance of life, it had also made them far more dangerous. They were willing and able to kill and she almost sensed their joy each time they took down a foe.

Working together, she and Loki cut down the entire pack of clones. When they were all dead, the daggers yanked themselves free from her hands. Landing on the ground, their pointed hilts became flexible. They used them like arms to drag themselves over to one of the fallen creatures, leaving small pock marks and drag lines from the tips of their blades to mark their journey.

Reaching the clone first, her right dagger tried to wipe itself clean on the creature's filthy loincloth. Instead of moving to another clone, the left dagger knocked its twin away and dragged its blade along the cloth. Taking offense, the right dagger slapped its sibling. Metal rang on metal as they descended into a slapping frenzy as they used their hilts to pummel each other.

"Am I really seeing this?" Ashley asked. She was in a daze from the attack, but seeing the daggers acting like naughty little children had pushed her to the edge.

"Cut it out, you two," Bianca said to her weapons. They froze, then seemed to realize they had an audience. The left dagger slunk over to another clone and they both cleaned themselves until they were satisfied all the blood was gone. They then dragged themselves over to their mistress. The right dagger used its hilt to point at the scuff marks on its blade.

"I think it wants to sharpen itself," Loki told her. He was long used to using magic, but even he'd never seen anything like this before.

Bianca took the whetstone out of her backpack and put it down between the daggers. "Play nice," she warned her weapons. Heeding her, they each chose a side and began scraping their blades along the edges. Bianca drew Loki away until she hoped they were out of earshot. "What did you do?" she hissed. Even Mack was disturbed by the daggers' behavior. He watched them warily while perched on Ashley's shoulder.

"I didn't think of the consequences," he replied in a low voice. "I just wondered what would happen if I infused them with my magic."

"Do you think its permanent?" Bianca asked.

They both looked at Mack, who cocked his head to the side as he stared at the newly animated weapons. "It would seem so," he replied. She put her hands over her face and he patted her on the shoulder consolingly. "Look on the bright side," he said cheerfully and waited for her to drop her hands before continuing. "At least you'll never have to clean or sharpen them again."

"Yeah, that's a real comfort," she said sarcastically. She turned to head back to the camp and winced at the pain in her ribs.

"You're hurt," Loki said and reached out to touch her on the arm. "How bad is it?"

"A few broken ribs," she replied and put her hand on the wounds. She frowned when she didn't feel the agony she'd expected. Twisting from side to side, she looked at Loki in confusion. "I could have sworn I felt them break when the clone punched me. Maybe it wasn't that bad after all."

"Broken ribs take weeks to heal," he said, glad she hadn't been wounded too badly. "You got off lucky."

"We all did," she said as they reached the camp. "I've never seen clones sneak up on anyone before. They're usually too stupid to think about using stealth."

"Perhaps they're evolving," Loki suggested. The snake that was supposed to have been their dinner was now a charred ruin. He doused the fire with a wave of his hand and left the burnt invertebrate in the ashes.

"Clones don't evolve," Bianca argued. "They haven't changed at all since the initial attack decades ago."

"Then I have no explanation as to why this pack attacked us in silence." Loki didn't like his lack of knowledge about this world. He knew very little about the beings who had invaded the planet, or its survivors. All he knew was that he and Bianca were the only ones who could use magic.

It hadn't been a coincidence that he'd fallen into her lap, so to speak. The visions he'd had of the two of them together backed up his theory. Clearly, the other versions of them meant something to each other. From the moment they'd first met, he'd felt a connection to her. Something had thrown them together and she was his best bet at finding a way off this dismal world.

Bianca knelt to pick up her daggers. They made no move to fight her as she placed them back in their sheaths. They'd gone dormant now that they didn't have anything to fight. Cleaning and sharpening themselves seemed to have soothed them to sleep.

"That was the weirdest thing I've ever seen," Ashley said as Loki and Bianca picked up their gear and they left the camp. "It's like they're alive now. How did that happen?"

"It was my fault," Loki admitted sheepishly. "It seems that if I use my magic on something that Bianca has animated, it becomes permanently altered."

"I don't think it would be a good idea for you to experiment like that again," Bianca said. "The daggers have a mind of their own and they fought me at first."

Loki felt guilty that she'd almost had her ribs broken because of what he'd done. She'd lost her concentration when she'd been trying to keep her weapons in line. She could have been killed because of his impulsive actions. He nodded his agreement and silently vowed not to infuse anything else on this planet with his magic. His curiosity could get them all killed if he didn't learn to curb his impulses.

Chapter Thirty-Two

It took them two more days to reach Danely. Loki spied it first. It hulked in the distance and he was disappointed to see it was just as derelict as Reaverton had been. He already knew they wouldn't find any help here, but they continued towards it anyway.

Vultures circled the city, indicating some sort of prey had to be here. When they were several miles from the ruins, they saw a mangled droid. Someone had beaten it to death with a blunt weapon.

They saw several more metal carcasses during their journey. It was late afternoon by the time they reached the outskirts of the ruins. They could hear the tortured clanking sounds of a unit of droids on the far side of the city. Soon, the clones would awaken and then they would begin their hunt.

"Do you want to stay here and try to find somewhere safe to hide from the clones, or do you want to leave?" Bianca asked. Now that they were a group, she preferred to get a general consensus rather than making their decisions for them.

"I vote for leaving," Ashley said. Her thin shoulders were shaking from fright and her dark eyes were huge. She'd never been so close to one of the ruined cities before. Everyone knew they were deathtraps and that it was safer to avoid them.

Loki's head whipped around when he heard something whistling through the air. He erected a shield a moment before an arrow splintered to pieces only an inch away from Ashley's nose.

Bianca drew her daggers and spun around to see someone sprinting towards them. It was a young man and his expression was intense as he raced towards Ashley. Murder was in his eyes that were startlingly similar to her mentor's. Whoever this boy was, he looked a lot like Tran Li. They had the same short, slender build and black hair.

Putting her daggers away, Bianca moved to intercept him. He attempted to dodge around her and she grabbed hold of his arm. Surprise flickered over his face when she tried to get him in an armlock. Dropping his bow, he threw a punch at her face. She blocked it and retaliated by issuing a front kick to his stomach. He leaped backwards and did a spinning side-kick that she barely managed to deflect. Tran Li had taught her well, but this boy was far better than she was.

"Did you know a man called Tran Li?" she asked before he could attack her again.

He froze in a fighting stance. "How do you know that name?" he demanded.

"He saved my life and taught me how to fight."

His eyes went to Ashley and hatred flared. "My uncle would never train raiders how to fight."

Loki stepped in front of the girl protectively. "Ashley is a victim of the raiders," he said. "She was forced to join them. We rescued her and she is one of us now."

Relaxing his stance a bit, the kid bent to pick up his bow. "Who are you?" he asked in a calmer tone. "Why are you here?"

Bianca did the introductions. "I'm Bianca. He's Loki, and that's Ashley." Mack poked his head over Ashley's shoulder. "That's Mack," she added.

The boy stumbled back a step, reaching for his bow again. "What the hell is that thing?" He knew it wasn't a real animal, which meant it had to be some kind of monster.

"He's my friend," Bianca said firmly. "He won't hurt you." Her daggers rattled in their sheaths. They'd woken up when she'd pulled them briefly and they were eager for blood.

"Who are you people?" the boy asked in bewilderment.

"We're travelers," Loki said smoothly. "We'd hoped to find people in Danely."

The kid shook his head dolefully. "All you will find here is droids and death." A howl rang through the ruins as the sun set and the first clone woke. "Not to mention clones," he added. "I am Zan Li, but you can call me Zan." He bowed and Bianca automatically bowed back. Zan eyed her with a glimmer of humor. "I see my uncle taught you manners." He made a gesture for them to follow him and turned towards the buildings. "I know a safe place where we can talk." Left with little choice now that the clones had awoken, they followed him into Danely.

Zan moved in enviable silence as he jogged through the streets. He avoided piles of rubble and it was apparent that he knew the city well. Reaching a building that had been gutted by fire, he ducked beneath a wide beam that blocked the way. The girls had no trouble navigating the small gap, but Loki had to crawl through, pushing his backpack ahead of himself.

"Sometimes, it pays to be small," Bianca said with a cheeky smile. Loki sent her a mock withering look that didn't intimidate her at all.

Zan paused at a heavy metal door and waited for them to catch up. He produced a key and unlocked it, then waited for them to enter before following them. He locked the door, plunging them into darkness. He hissed out a curse when light bloomed as a magical white globe appeared.

"It won't hurt you," Bianca hasted to reassure him.

Ashley was gaping at the light as well. "Did you create that?" she asked Bianca.

"No," Loki replied. "It's mine."

Zan backed away until he hit the door. "You are both witches?" he asked, eyes darting between Bianca and Loki.

"Relax," Ashley said soothingly. "They're not evil like all the stories say. They're just like us, except they can do a few neat tricks."

Licking his lips nervously, it was obvious he didn't believe her. "How do I know you won't kill me and use my body for your perverted spells?"

Bianca snorted out a laugh. "I don't even know any spells. I can just animate stuff."

"If anyone is perverted between the two of us, it would be me," Loki said dryly. "I know many spells, but none that involve dead bodies."

"Can we please find somewhere to sit down?" Ashley asked plaintively. "I'm exhausted."

Zan studied them all, then reached a decision. "My home isn't far now," he said and took the lead. He was intrigued by the small band of strangers, but he was also terrified. Like everyone, he'd been raised to believe magic was evil. Only the fact that his uncle had apparently saved the witch calling herself Bianca stopped him from running. He'd thought his uncle was dead and he wanted to know how he'd come to train a dreaded magic user to fight.

A set of stairs took them to what had once been a boiler room. Electricity had died along with most of the population and the machines no longer worked. He took a confusing series of tunnels, then led them down more stairs to a final hallway. Another locked door awaited at the end. He fished another key out and opened it. With a bow, he gestured for his guests to enter first. "Welcome to my home," he said formally. It had been years since he'd last spoken to other humans, but he hadn't forgotten his manners.

Loki entered first with his hand on his sword, ready to draw it at a moment's notice. He didn't see any threats and indicated that it was safe. The girls followed him inside and Zan closed and locked the door. He'd left a lamp burning and it softly illuminated a motley collection of old furniture. Several chairs had been arranged around his fire, which was banked at the moment. He'd collected pots and pans to use for cooking and utensils as well. He had a small bed in a corner of the room and a few books for entertainment.

"This is nice," Ashley said in surprise. "It's better than my old cave."

"What do you do for water?" Bianca asked.

Zan pointed at a huge wooden barrel near the fire. "I collect it from a nearby cave and store it here. I have to boil it before I can use it, but it doesn't taste too bad."

They all took a seat around the banked fire, then he offered them water from a bottle. They each took a few sips and handed it back. He took a seat as well and folded his hands on his lap. "How do you know my uncle?" he asked now that the pleasantries had been completed.

Bianca took a deep breath, then launched into her story.

Chapter Thirty-Three

Zan stared blankly into the coals of the fire when Bianca finished telling him about her history with his uncle. It was a lot of information to process for someone who had been alone for as long as he had.

"Tran Li thought he was the only one who had survived the attack on his village," Bianca said after a few moments of silence. "He wouldn't have left if he'd known you'd also survived."

Zan gave her a distracted smile. "I know. My uncle was very honorable." He wished he'd known there had been another survivor. He would have followed his uncle to the far ends of the earth rather than live here all alone.

"How did you survive?" Ashley asked him tentatively. She hadn't forgotten that she'd been his target. With her hair, tattoo and clothing, she couldn't be mistaken for anything other than a raider. It would take her months to grow her hair out enough to cover the tattoo. In the meantime, she would have to find something less torn and raggedy to wear. Her mother had taught her how to sew, so all she needed was some material. She could fashion something wearable quickly enough.

"I'd been sent to get water," Zan said quietly. "Our cavern only had one spring and it was barely enough for our family of twelve to survive. We needed to get our washing water from another nearby cave." He took a breath as he remembered the tragedy from so long ago. "Uncle Tran was out hunting at the time. He must have returned before I did and saw the slaughter. There were so many body parts lying around that it would have been impossible to tell I wasn't among the pile."

"You came back to find everyone dead?" Bianca asked in sympathy.

He nodded sadly. "Like my uncle, I thought everyone had been killed. I stumbled across the raiders' tracks several miles away and followed them to their camp. There were over forty of them and they'd taken one of my cousins with them." Tears gathered in his eyes and he blinked them away. "She was already half dead by the time I found them. She died from blood loss while I watched and I could do nothing to save her."

Bianca and Ashley shuddered at the fate the poor girl had suffered. "What did you do?" Ashley asked.

"My father taught me how to hunt with a bow and knives," Zan replied. "Like Bianca, my uncle Tran taught myself and my cousins how to fight with our hands and feet. I followed the raiders and picked them off one by one, being careful not to be seen." He smiled faintly at the memory. "They thought they were being haunted by a vengeful spirit and they were right. By the time I finally finished them off, I'd left my cave far behind. Danely was the closest settlement that could offer me shelter. I found this place and made it my home. For the past seven years, I've slowly been whittling down the number of droids that infest the ruins."

"How old were you when your family was killed?" Bianca asked.

"Twelve," he replied.

"You're only a year older than me," Ashley said. Empathy filled her face. "My whole family was slaughtered by the raiders who took me," she added.

"They must have abused you horribly." He was ashamed that he'd automatically thought she was evil just from the way she looked. She'd suffered just as much as he had.

"They were female," she said and his head jerked in surprise. "They took over a town and enslaved the men."

"That's a switch," he murmured. He could barely take his eyes off her now that he knew she was just a normal girl. She was very pretty beneath the grime and he'd been alone for far too long.

Loki rolled his eyes and Bianca sent him a warning look not to ruin their moment. They both knew a romance was brewing between the teens. He huffed out a quiet sigh, but obeyed her wish and kept his mouth shut.

Zan tore his eyes away from Ashley and contemplated his guests solemnly. "Do you believe in destiny?" he asked.

Loki sniggered quietly and Bianca frowned at him reprovingly. "Not really," she replied. "Why do you ask?"

"My people believe that some are chosen for greatness. It can be a great honor, but it is also a heavy burden." His gaze came to rest on Bianca. "You are the descendent of Whitney Caldwell, the witch who was supposed to rescue us and who ultimately failed her duty. The burden has fallen to you to fix her mistakes and to save this world."

"Why does everyone keep saying that?" Bianca complained. "Just because I can use magic doesn't mean I'm a hero."

"You are not a champion yet," Zan agreed. "But you could become one, if you choose to be."

They all stared at her and even Loki was watching her for her reaction. He sensed this was a pivotal moment and that his future hung in the balance.

"What do you expect me to do?" Bianca said in exasperation. "Singlehandedly kill every droid and clone on the planet?"

"Accepting your destiny is the first step," Zan said. "Everything will fall into place once you no longer fight your fate."

He sounded far too wise for a nineteen-year-old kid and she scowled. "Tran Li never tried to force me to be a savior."

Zan gave her an enigmatic smile. "No. He just trained you to be a warrior. Why did he teach you the skills that have never been shown to anyone outside of our family before, I wonder?"

"Because he was bored?" she said sarcastically. "He never said why he was teaching me. I assumed it was to help him hunt for food and to help me learn how to hide from the clones and droids." Not to mention the civilians who had evicted her from their cavern.

"Perhaps he saw the same potential in you that I do," Zan said. "You can change the fate of this world, but you won't have to do it alone."

"Yeah, we three will help you," Ashley said. Her eyes were shining with excitement. Mack poked her in the arm indignantly. "I mean, we *four* will help you," she corrected herself and the monkey grinned at her.

"I was thinking of someone far better trained and better equipped than us," the boy said.

"Who do you have in mind?" Loki queried. He could see the kid had a plan, but he didn't trust him yet and he wanted to learn more.

"When I was hunting for food a few weeks ago, I discovered a small group of travelers. They were settlers rather than raiders, so I left them in peace. I overheard them talking about a city they were heading towards. They mentioned that it was run by the remnants of the military."

"Soldiers," Bianca mused. It was possible they could have maintained their training and that they could be in possession of guns. "It couldn't hurt to check them out, I guess. Where is their city?"

"I heard it will take us roughly three weeks to walk there," Zan replied and Ashley groaned. "We will have a better chance of reaching it in a group than if we were to travel alone."

"You're coming with us?" Loki asked.

Zan gave him a short nod. "You were put in my path for a reason. It is my destiny to join you."

Bianca didn't really believe in fate, but she wasn't about to turn away someone with his skills. He'd survived alone for seven years, proving he was tough and intelligent. He would be a valuable ally. He was also an accomplished hunter and could help feed their strange crew during the long journey ahead.

Chapter Thirty-Four

Zan prepared a stew and Loki started the fire beneath the pot with a click of his fingers. The teen widened his eyes slightly, but that was the only sign of nervousness he gave at the display of magic. He was going to have to get used to it if he planned to join their group.

"I don't suppose you have any spare clothes I could modify to fit me?" Ashley asked tentatively.

Zan eyed her tall, thin frame and indicated for her to follow him. "You're taller than me, but I think I have something that might be suitable."

They stood and she followed him to a corner where he kept his belongings. He sorted through a small pile of clothing and handed over a shirt and pants. Standing side by side, she was two inches taller than him. Their height difference didn't seem to bother either of them as they stole glances at each other. "Do you have any sewing supplies?" she asked.

"I have some," Bianca said and fished inside her backpack. She'd kept the needle and thread in a front pocket, knowing they would come in handy sooner or later.

Ashley crossed to her, took the items and sat down. She didn't need to measure the shirt and pants to adjust them to fit her. She'd been making her own clothing for the past few years. It was a skill that was highly prized in her cave.

Humming beneath her breath, she quickly made a few alterations to the shirt so it wouldn't be as bulky on her wiry frame. She let the hem of the pants down and took in the waist. There wasn't much cotton left when she was done, but she was happy with the results. She stripped down to her threadbare underwear and pulled the new clothes on. Zan stared at her, mesmerized by her slender form until she covered herself again. "How do I look?" she asked and posed for them.

"Beautiful," Zan said, then blushed brightly. "I mean, you don't look as much like a reaver now. Once your hair grows out, you'll look like a normal civilian again."

They opted to rest for the night and the next day and left Danely at mid-afternoon. They wanted to be well clear of the ruins before the clones woke. Zan's efforts to whittle down the droids meant there were fewer here and they were easy to avoid. Their scanners only worked at close range, so they made sure to keep a wide berth whenever they heard clomping footsteps.

They were all loaded up with supplies. Zan had distributed his store of water in flasks and they all carried their share. Bianca's load felt strangely light, so she offered to carry some of Ashley's for her. The younger woman gladly handed over a couple of flasks. She wasn't used to walking for so long every day and carrying such a heavy load, but she knew she would toughen up eventually.

They hiked away from the ruins, heading eastward towards the town where the soldiers were rumored to be. Loki mused about his choice to head towards Danely. It had stood out to him on the map, but he couldn't say why. He could have chosen to head to one of the other cities. It almost felt as though he was being guided. He hated the idea of not being the master of his own decisions. No one had the right to use him as their puppet.

He didn't conjure up a magical globe as they hiked. The moon was half-full, giving them plenty of light to see where they were going. As always, the temperature dropped sharply when the sun went down. Constantly being on the move would keep them warm enough. He mused about the adventure he'd found himself on. It was almost nice to have companions, even if they were three lowly humans and an animated toy monkey. Mack was riding on his shoulder, keeping a vigilant watch for enemies. As was his habit, his tail was wrapped securely around Loki's neck.

Seeing a grin playing around Loki's mouth, Bianca wondered what was on his mind, but she didn't have the courage to ask. This all seemed to be a game to him. This wasn't his world and he wasn't invested in its survival. He just wanted to find a way home. That was her plan as well, but she'd somehow been roped into attempting to save Earth. Privately, she was planning to escape as soon as she found a way out. She didn't owe this planet anything. Its inhabitants shunned and despised her. They'd even tried to kill her several times. Why the hell should she try to save them?

She kept these thoughts to herself as they trekked through the night. They stopped to rest at dawn and Ashley fell into a deep sleep. Zan lay down near her and he also fell into a doze. Loki and Bianca walked a short distance away so they wouldn't wake the pair when they spoke. Neither were particularly tired yet despite their long walk.

"They'll make a cute couple," Loki said with a sly look at the youngsters.

"They deserve to have someone to care about," Bianca replied absently. She stared up at the stars, wondering how far away Asgard was and whether Loki would ever be able to return to his home.

"Do you believe Zan's theory?" he asked. "That we're being guided by an unknown entity?"

She turned to face him and saw he was being serious for once. "Not really. I think we make our own destinies."

"I always thought that, too," he agreed, but his tone held a hint of doubt.

"But you don't now?" she prodded.

He hesitated, then shifted his stance slightly. "I'm not sure. I think there have been a few too many coincidences since you first saved me. I'm beginning to feel as if I'm being manipulated."

"By what?"

"That I don't know," he replied darkly. "I do not like the sensation of being someone's servant."

"Neither do I," she agreed. "Will it be worth it if the invisible puppet master can help us find a way to get you home?"

"I suppose," he replied reluctantly. "I can't help but wonder what their motive is."

"We already know what they want from us," she said. "We have to save this world."

"Perhaps you are right," he said with a speculative gleam in his eyes. "If I assist you in this endeavor, finding my way home could be my reward."

She rolled her eyes inwardly that all he could think about was himself. It never occurred to him to wonder what her reward would be, or what benefit their new companions could receive from this endeavor. He was the most conceited person she'd ever met, but it probably wasn't his fault. He'd been raised to think the universe revolved around him.

"Come on, your Worship," she said quietly. "We should try to get some rest."

Raising his brows at her snarky tone, Loki wondered what he'd done to deserve her ire this time. Women were a puzzle he knew he'd never be able to solve. He followed her back to their temporary camp and lay down on the hard ground a few feet away from her.

He closed his eyes, but his mind was buzzing and he found it hard to sleep. From Bianca's restless shifting, she was also having trouble resting. They should have both been exhausted, but he felt as though he could have walked forever. He'd noticed the wound on her temple had healed without a trace of a scar, but she didn't seem to realize it yet. The cut on his lip had also disappeared. Something strange was going on, but he wasn't about to complain about it. Increased stamina and healing abilities surely couldn't be a bad thing.

Chapter Thirty-Five

Following the ancient train tunnels, they opted to remain above ground where they could see danger coming. They neared what had once been a large town after a few days of travel. It was midmorning, so they weren't in danger of being attacked by clones. Droids tended to patrol the ruined cities rather than smaller settlements like this.

"I wonder if we could scrounge up some canvas from in there?" Ashley said as they stood on the edge of the derelict town.

"Sick of the four of us being squeezed in the tiny two-man tent already?" Loki said teasingly.

"Yeah," she replied with a cheeky grin. "No offense, but you and Zan smell."

"We aren't too fresh either," Bianca reminded her dryly. They were all in dire need of a bath, but they hadn't come across an underground spring yet. Their water was too precious to waste on bathing.

"It looks clear," Zan said. He'd been scouring the town for signs of movement ever since they'd spotted it. His senses were highly attuned after being on his own for so long. He took the lead, holding his bow with an arrow ready to be drawn and aimed at a target.

Ashley picked her way over the rubble, following closely behind Zan. Bianca went next and Loki brought up the rear. He should have been watching for trouble, but he was having a hard time tearing his gaze away from Bianca's bewitching form. Even when she was dusty from travel, she was gorgeous. Her hair shone with hints of fire and her slender body was becoming more enticing by the day. If he didn't know better, he might have believed that she'd cast a spell over him. By her own admission, her magic didn't work that way. It was her natural feminine allure than had ensnared him so deeply in her clutches.

Feeling Loki's eyes on her, Bianca refused to turn around and catch him in the act of ogling her butt again. He'd always been flirty, but he'd become more intense since they'd infused her daggers with his magic. He watched her constantly and she felt herself being drawn to him by his sheer charisma.

He was easily the most handsome man she'd ever seen, but there was more to him than mere good-looks. He was intelligent, witty and funny, but he could also be cutting, sarcastic and, of course, highly selfish. She would have to be crazy to let herself have feelings for him and she was determined not to fall for his charm. He was a magician and she couldn't even be sure if his appeal was real, or if it was fabricated.

Zan searched the town and spied a building that had tattered fabric caught in a smashed window. He and Ashley ventured inside while Bianca and Loki stood guard. Ashley found some sheets of canvas that were in fairly good condition. Zan helped her find sewing supplies and they stuffed the items into a large canvas bag.

"How long will it take you to make a tent out of that?" Loki asked.

"A couple of hours," Ashley replied. "It won't be much good without metal poles, though."

They scavenged some more until Zan found some old curtain rods in a decrepit house. He gathered up enough to make a frame for the tent, then they exited from the town and travelled some distance from it. When they were roughly halfway to the next station, Loki called a halt. Lighting a fire at night was risky and the sun would fall in a couple more hours. They were running low on food and he wanted to hunt while the teens were busy. "May I borrow your bow and arrows?" he asked Zan.

"You know how to use them?" the kid asked in surprise.

"I should hope so," Loki replied with a grin. "I've been hunting game for over a millennia."

"How long is that?" Ashley asked with a curious expression.

"It's over a thousand years," Bianca told her. "Loki is a lot older than he looks."

The kids gaped at him while Zan handed over his bow. Loki pulled the quiver full of arrows over his shoulder and expertly drew the string back to test it. "This is well-made," he complimented Zan. "It should do nicely." He turned to look at Bianca and cocked his eyebrow. "Do you feel like hunting coyote with me?" He'd heard their yips and howls in the distance and knew a pack was somewhere in the area. It was high time he showed her he wasn't as useless as she seemed to believe he was. He'd learned to adapt to his environment and now knew not to leave tracks their enemies could follow. If he could hunt deer, he shouldn't have any trouble tracking some dogs.

Bianca wasn't about to miss out on seeing him hunt and went with him. Mack opted to remain with the teens. He was fascinated with their project of creating another tent. He sat on Ashley's shoulder and watched as she spread the canvas out on the ground.

Loki kept his pace to one Bianca could keep up with and strode towards the coyote pack. There was no wind to carry their scent to their prey and betray their presence. They closed in on the animals to see they'd found a meal of their own. Most were busy eating their kill. A lone coyote stood watch with its back to them. Loki nocked an arrow, sighted and let fly. It hit the sentry in the back of its neck and it went down with a yelp.

Breaking away from their meal of what looked like the carcass of a vulture, the rest of the pack zeroed in on the interlopers. Snarling in fury, they raced towards the beings who had dared to kill one of their brothers.

Loki took three of the beasts down with arrows. Bianca pulled her daggers and they came alive in her hands. Instead of fighting her, they quivered, eager to spill blood. She drew her arms back to her shoulders, then flicked them towards the remaining two coyotes. Following her mental command, they changed their trajectory in mid-air and dipped down to spear into the chests of the sprinting animals.

"Nicely done," Loki complimented her as the beasts fell. "You've gained control of the daggers."

"Only when I need them to kill something," she said wryly as they crossed to the fallen coyotes. Her daggers had pulled themselves free of the corpses and were wiping their blades on the fur to clean themselves.

"They're fastidious little fellows," Loki noted. Although the daggers liked to kill, they seemed to dislike being dirty.

"I think that's because Tran Li taught me to always clean my weapons when I was finished with them," Bianca said. He'd found them in Reaverton and had given them to her when he'd begun to train her. "I must have passed that on to them when we animated them." Loki had probably cemented the command when he'd mixed his magic with hers.

They waited patiently until the daggers were satisfied that they were clean. The right Sai made an imperious gesture at Bianca and she heaved a small sigh. She'd known they would feel compelled to sharpen themselves and had brought her whetstone along. She took it out of her pocket and dropped it to the ground.

Loki sauntered over to the animals he'd killed and retrieved Zan's arrows. They were still in good condition, so he wiped them clean and put them back in the quiver. He chose the least bloody coyote and heaved it over his shoulder. The daggers had finished sharpening themselves by the time he returned to Bianca. She knelt to retrieve them, giving him a perfect view straight down her shirt.

His eyes remained on her cleavage as she straightened up. She gave him a withering stare when he managed to drag his gaze up to her face. "Shall we?" he said with a winning smile and gestured towards their camp. Shaking her head, Bianca preceded him. He didn't mind at all. Not when the view from behind was just as good as it was from the front.

Chapter Thirty-Six

Bianca butchered the coyote and Loki cooked it over the fire. She used some of her own water to wash her hands and arms. She didn't need to drink as much now. Her body must have adjusted to travelling through the harsh desert. That had to be the reason why she didn't feel as hungry or thirsty, or seem to need as much sleep now. Loki had also adjusted to the conditions. Ashley was still struggling, but she was fairly new to the life of a nomad. Zan had fit into their group seamlessly. He was well-used to having short supplies of food.

By the time the sun left the sky, Ashley had made a new tent and Zan had fashioned poles to prop it up. It was almost an exact match for her original tent. Now they wouldn't have to cram four people inside just one. Loki took possession of the new tent and shouldered the second backpack. Zan insisted on carrying the original tent so Ashley was no longer burdened with it.

"We need to find fresh water soon," Bianca said as Loki doused the campfire. They had enough food to last them for a few days before they would need to hunt again.

"I'm sure we will come across a cave soon," Zan said. "This area is riddled with them."

"How will we know when we're near one?" Ashley asked.

"They're usually near cliffs and gorges. There will also be more signs of plant life than usual."

"You mean other than cacti?" she said dryly. They were the only types of plants that still thrived in the desert after the alien gas. Small, wiry bushes had been in the area near her old cavern, but she hadn't seen anything like that so far. He flashed her a quick grin and she smiled in return.

"Ah, young love," Loki murmured quietly to Bianca. "Was your romance with Sean this sweet to watch as it unfolded?"

"There was no romance between us," she said flatly.

"He was your first boyfriend, I take it?" Loki asked.

"He was my only boyfriend. The other boys were afraid of me and he was the only one who wanted me."

"Why wasn't he afraid, I wonder?"

"I think he was kind of obsessed with me," she replied. "He used to stare at me when we were kids. He snuck me food when his parents weren't watching. We rarely spoke, but he was the closest thing I had to a friend."

Loki felt pity swell even as he battled his jealousy of the boy she'd once dated. "Why did he turn on you if he was so obsessed with you?"

"Remember when I told you my magic took a big leap soon after I turned fourteen?"

He nodded. "You didn't tell me exactly what happened to you."

"It was just after Sean and I slept together for the first and only time," she said. Again, it hadn't been her choice. The decision had been made for her and she hadn't had any say in it. Loki stiffened in surprise at that revelation, but she continued her story. "He was rough and hurt me badly enough that I think I went into shock. When he tried to touch me again, I panicked. I grabbed my shirt and animated it, then threw it at him. It wrapped tightly around his face and he tried to pull it away, but it was too strong. His screams were muffled and I'm pretty sure it would have smothered him to death if my magic hadn't faded after I ran."

Loki sucked in a breath at what she'd endured. She'd only been fourteen when her so called boyfriend had used her young body. He'd traumatized her, then had turned against her when she'd rejected him. "You should have let him suffocate," he said in a low, hard tone. "If I'd known what he'd done to you, I would have killed him myself."

"I don't think he knew what he was doing. I was his first, too."

"There is no excuse for hurting a woman while engaging in sex," he said tightly. "Not that you were a woman at the time. You were just a child when he brutalized you."

She reached out to touch his hand in warning when the teens glanced over their shoulders at his tone. "It happened a long time ago and I'm fine now," she said. Physically, she'd healed, but the mental scars still remained.

"Do you ever intend to let another man sleep with you again?" he asked. The horror on her face said it all. "You are not fine," he told her. "Instead of initiating you into the wonders and pleasures of sex, he turned it into an ordeal that you have no wish to repeat." He took a deep breath, then entwined his fingers with hers. "Sex isn't painful if it is done with care," he told her in a much gentler tone. "I will make it my mission to personally show you how pleasurable it can be."

He smiled down at her and she was mesmerized by his brilliant blue eyes. "That won't be necessary," she said and tore her gaze away from his face. "I'll take your word for it."

"But I insist," he said silkily. "You saw in our shared vision how good we can be together."

"They were other versions of us," she retorted and pulled her hand free. "I don't need a demonstration and I prefer to be left alone."

"We'll see about that," he murmured to himself as she hurried to catch up to the others.

Mack leaped onto her shoulder and saw she was rattled. He sent Loki a suspicious glare, but he just smiled. Now that he knew how badly Bianca had suffered, he was determined to rectify it. No woman should go through life thinking sex was to be feared. He intended to teach her that it should be revered. All he had to do was find somewhere private, then somehow get her naked. His hands, mouth and body would do the rest.

Chapter Thirty-Seven

They were running dangerously low on water by the time Zan spotted a cavern. They'd found an old riverbed and had followed it for a few miles. It deviated from their route, but they wouldn't be able to make it to their destination without stocking up on supplies.

It was just before midday, so if any clones were living in the cave, they would sleep for a few more hours. They quietly moved to the mouth of the small cavern and listened intently.

"I don't hear anything," Zan whispered. "I'll scout the tunnels to make sure it is safe."

"Can you see in the dark?" Loki asked dryly. When the kid hesitated, he conjured up a magic globe and sent it on ahead.

"We'll all go," Bianca said. "I don't want us to become separated until we know it's safe." She went first and Loki was right on her heels. His globe lit the way, keeping pace with her. It hovered a few feet above her head so it didn't shine directly in her eyes. She drew her daggers and they began to quiver in her hands in suppressed excitement at the possibility of action.

The long tunnel ended in a small cavern with two tunnels branching off at the back. From the signs of an old campfire, someone had lived here long ago. Human bones were scattered around the ground. A shattered skull grinned at them toothlessly. It was so small that it had to have belonged to a child.

"That poor family," Ashley said. Zan put his arm around her shoulder and she slipped her hand around his waist.

"I can't see any recent remains," Bianca said as she examined the cave. It seemed clones had found the humans and had killed and eaten them before moving on. They explored the other two tunnels. One led to the surface and would act as an escape route if needed. The other led to a larger cavern with a deep spring that was a good twenty feet wide. She knelt to taste the water and deemed it to be drinkable. The spring would be large enough for them to bathe and wash their clothing. Ashley had made them all spare sets from material she'd scrounged along the way.

"It should be safe for us to rest here for a bit," Bianca decided. "We need to hunt for more food to last us for the rest of the journey."

"I love it when you take charge," Loki said with a smirk. "You're so small, yet so bossy."

"Someone has to be the leader, your Highness," she said with a smirk of her own. "I'm sure you wouldn't want to sully your delicate hands with the job."

He pursed his lips and looked at his grimy hands. His fingernails were cracked and encrusted with filth. "It is a bit late for that, I'm afraid."

"Besides," she added, "I wouldn't want the power to go to your head. Knowing your history, you might try to take over our world."

She was just joking, but the barb hit him and he winced. "I assure you, I have no wish to rule over this decaying planet and its raggedy inhabitants."

"I see why you call him 'your Highness' now," Zan said with a dark look at Loki. "He really does think he's better than us."

"Can you perform magic and do you have a life expectancy of several thousand years?" Loki retorted. At their confounded expressions, he smiled smugly. "Exactly," he said in self-satisfaction.

Ashley turned to Bianca in wonder. "Are you going to live for thousands of years, too?"

"Me?" Bianca replied in surprise. "No. Why would I?"

"Because you can use magic, too."

"So could my great-grandmother," Bianca reminded her. "I hear she was in her twenties when she died."

"Oh, I can die," Loki said. "It isn't easy to kill my kind, but it is possible." He looked Bianca up and down with a hint of pity. "You are human, so you will age and die as all your kind do."

"Why do your people live for so long?" Zan asked.

"We have trees that bear magical apples. They prolong our lives as long as we feed on their fruit once a century or so."

"Lucky you," Ashley muttered. It was no wonder Loki considered himself to be superior to them. From everything he'd just said, he came from a species that were god-like.

"Tell them your title," Bianca said with a hint of a grin.

"I am known as the God of Mischief," he said and flourished a pretend cape.

"Why doesn't that surprise me?" Zan murmured.

"You're a god?" Ashley asked, frightened that her idle thought might actually be accurate.

"Of course not," Bianca said with a snort. "He's no more a god than I am."

Loki put a hand over his heart. "You wound me. It was humans who gave us our titles so long ago, after all."

"I think it's time you had a new title," she retorted. "I'm thinking 'God of Vanity' suits you far better."

"Insolent girl," he said with a sniff. "I shall thrash you soundly for that." She was still holding her daggers and they suddenly jerked towards him. "I was just jesting, of course," he said, raising his hands to show he meant her no harm.

"Down, boys," Bianca said to her weapons and sheathed them before they could drag her over to Loki and make her stab him. "It looks like you'll need to watch what you say around them," she warned him.

"So it would appear," he agreed.

"We can wash later," Bianca decided and they trooped back to the smaller cave. "Loki and Zan, head out and try to bring back a couple of coyotes. Ashley and I will set up camp."

Loki saluted her sarcastically. "You speak and we obey, oh Mistress of Skepticism."

She sniggered at the title she'd given herself, surprised he'd remembered it. The men left through the main entrance and she and Ashley cleared away the bones that littered the campsite.

They piled more rocks around the campfire, then set up a small pot to make tea. Another far larger pot would hold stew. They'd managed to find some plants along the way that they could add to the mix. Vegetables were so rare that they'd had to adapt and eat whatever greenery wouldn't poison them.

Ashley sipped her tea with a troubled expression. "Is something wrong?" Bianca asked.

"What do you think of Zan?" Ashley asked.

"He seems like a decent guy. Why?" Bianca already knew the answer, but Ashley needed to talk and it was rare for them to be alone. Mack had gone hunting with the boys, so it was just the girls left.

"I have…feelings for him that I've never felt before," the younger woman confessed. "I've been with boys from my cave, but none of them made me warm inside like he does." Seeing Bianca's cheeks go slightly pink, she gave her a knowing look. "It's kind of like how Loki makes you feel, I'd say."

"He doesn't make me feel warm," Bianca refuted.

"How does he make you feel, then?"

"Conflicted," Bianca replied softly.

"You want him, but you don't want to want him," Ashley summed up. She was wise for someone who was still so young.

"Something like that," Bianca said with a sigh. "At least Zan thinks you're his equal."

Ashley's expression turned vulnerable. "Do you think he likes me?"

"I know he does. I see the way he looks at you when he thinks you aren't aware of it."

"You mean the way you and Loki look at each other?" Ashley said slyly. Bianca gave her a stern frown, but she wasn't going to be put off. "He might be an ancient being from another world, but he likes you and you like him. Our lives are short and mostly full of misery. What's wrong with taking pleasure where you can find it?"

"Nothing, I guess," Bianca replied. Pleasure was a foreign concept to her when it came to men. "Is that why you weren't married before Silvia and her gang killed everyone in your cave? You wanted to have fun first?"

"There wasn't much of a choice of partners where I used to live," Ashley said, wrinkling her nose. "I was taller than most of the boys. None of them wanted to have a wife that towered over them. We met up a few times a year with people from other caves in the area. I was going to marry a boy I met a couple of years ago, but he was killed while hunting."

She took a sip of tea, but she didn't seem particularly sad. Love was rare in this reality. People married out of necessity and to attempt to repopulate the Earth. Romance was largely a thing of the past. Seeing how attracted Ashley and Zan were to each other, Bianca knew they could have something special if only they were given time to nurture their relationship. While she and Loki felt an attraction to each other, they couldn't have a lasting connection. He belonged on Asgard and she highly doubted she would even be welcome there.

Chapter Thirty-Eight

Loki and Zan returned just before nightfall. "We have brought you two coyotes, as ordered," Loki said as he and Zan dumped the dead beasts on the ground next to the fire. "Now, if you have no objections, I'm going to wash up."

"You may leave," Bianca said with an imperious wave of her hand. Ashley giggled and Zan's usually inscrutable face cracked into a small smile. "Why don't you both wash up?" she added. "Make sure you clean your clothes, too."

Loki heaved a put-upon sigh. "You sound like my ex-wife, Sigyn. She could be quite a harridan at times." Turning to Zan, he clapped the boy on the shoulder. "Come, young man, let us perform our menial duties before Bianca gives us a tongue lashing." They bent to retrieve their backpacks and he sent Bianca a look over his shoulder. His expression suggested he wouldn't have minded a tongue lashing from her at all.

"That man…" Bianca said in frustration and trailed off.

"Has it bad for you," Ashley finished for her, then descended into giggles. "I bet you'd love it if he gave you a tongue lashing," she added.

Mack looked from Bianca to Ashley and back again, clearly confused by their discussion. He scratched his head, then scampered off after the boys.

Muttering beneath her breath, Bianca drew her right dagger. It remained dormant as she skinned both animals and gutted them. Ashley helped her to clean up the mess. They left the discarded bits a safe distance away from their temporary campground.

When they returned to the fire, they found the boys were back and were cutting the animals into manageable pieces. Loki wasn't used to this kind of work and was learning as he went. They lay strips on a rock and he conjured up fire to dry them. The rest went into the stewpot.

"I'm going to wash up," Ashley said, since it looked like they had everything under control.

"I'll take my turn later," Bianca said. She preferred to be alone when she bathed.

"Be careful," Zan said. "The spring is very deep in the center."

"Thanks for the warning." Ashley smiled flirtatiously and his eyes remained glued to her as she took a torch and headed for the tunnel that led to the spring.

Loki exchanged a look with Bianca. They both knew it was only a matter of time before the teens snuck off to have some alone time. He hoped they wouldn't eventually end up having a lover's spat. That would make things awkward for their small group.

Checking on the stew, Bianca was satisfied that it tasted okay. The spring water had a slightly metallic flavor, but it didn't detract from their meal too much. Loki sat closely beside her. His shoulder-length hair still dripped and he'd slicked it back from his face. Squeaky clean, he was undeniably handsome. Aware of Zan's scrutiny, she resolutely kept her attention on her task. She was their leader, at least for now, and she wasn't about to act like a giddy little girl.

Ashley returned a while later with her freshly scrubbed clothes and lay them over rocks to dry along with the other soaked garments. "I'm glad you warned me about the pool," she said to Zan. "It's a lot deeper than it looks."

He inclined his head in a nod, apparently speechless. She wore a sleeveless shirt and he caught glimpses of her worn bra and flawless skin whenever she moved her arms.

Loki rolled his eyes, wishing the pair would just get naked together so the sexual tension could finally ease. Catching Bianca's gaze on him, he had to admit that they were just as bad. He ached to have her in his arms and he wasn't sure how much longer he could wait. He'd been abstinent for far too long and his body was determined to be satiated.

After dinner, they each chose a place to make their bed. They banked the fire and lay down to sleep. Bianca waited until everyone was breathing deeply before she snuck away. Apart from in a dream, she'd never been fully submerged in water and she wasn't sure how she was going to react to it. She didn't want anyone to witness it if she panicked. Mack rose to follow her, but she motioned for him to remain behind.

Transferring a few coals from the fire into a pot, she used the faint embers to light her way as she made her way to the spring. She stripped naked and washed her clothes thoroughly, then squeezed the water out and spread them out on the ground. Scooting closer to the water, she eased into it and found it to be shallow near the edge.

When she sat down, it was only waist deep. Just as she'd suspected, it frightened her to have so much water surrounding her. It took her a few minutes to adjust to the sensation. Using the soap Ashley had made, she washed the grime from her body. Lying back, she dunked her hair until it was soaked, then washed it as well.

The sensation of water sliding all over her body was more sensual than she'd expected. She rinsed her hair, then luxuriated in the experience of her first real bath.

Memories of the dream she'd had of Loki being in an actual tub with her resurfaced. She could almost feel his hands on her right now.

Taking a deep, shuddering breath, she stood up. The pool slanted slightly downwards and moss covered the area she was standing in. Her feet slipped and she fell backwards. The ground disappeared and it was too dark to see. Swallowing water, she splashed around, trying to find the edge. Blind panic set in as she flailed around. The others were asleep and she was too far away for them to hear if she called for help.

A small part of her was amazed at the irony that she was going to drown while being in the middle of a desert. The rest of her was terrified. Her friends all seemed to expect her to save the world, but it seemed she couldn't even save herself.

Chapter Thirty-Nine

Loki lay on his makeshift bed with his hands behind his head. He wasn't tired yet, but Bianca had insisted on them all bedding down. He watched her without alerting her that he was still awake when she quietly got up after an hour or so. She gathered coals from the fire to make a crude light, then grabbed her laundry. For reasons only she knew, it appeared she wanted to make very sure she wouldn't be disturbed when she bathed.

He wanted to gain her trust, so he remained behind even though he desperately wanted to join her. He watched the tunnel that led to the spring expectantly and began to frown when she didn't return. Filled with an urgent need to check on her, he rose silently and trotted towards the spring. He didn't bother to create a light and relied on his night vision to guide him.

Hearing splashing noises and the sounds of distress ahead, he gave up his attempt at being stealthy and took off at a run. He conjured a light and threw it high into the air. Bianca was in the middle of the spring where the water was far deeper than at the edges. Her head went under and he leaped into the small pool.

Bianca's panic increased when hands grabbed her around the waist. In her terror, she thought the souls of the damned were dragging her downwards to hell. Her head broke the surface and she coughed out water.

"Shh, I've got you," a husky voice said into her ear.

"Loki?" she said. Her throat was sore from shouting.

"You're safe now," he replied. "I'd never let anything bad happen to you." He realized he was babbling and clenched his teeth shut as he swam over to the edge. Bianca's eyes were huge and had turned green with terror. She was shivering and he pulled her onto his lap. He held her tightly to his chest and she wrapped her arms around his neck.

"You saved me," she said in a small voice.

"I thought it was time I repaid the favor," he replied.

She could hear the smirk in his voice, but she knew it was just a cover. She'd seen his concern and knew that it was real. When she pulled back, he stroked a hand down her back soothingly. They both became aware that she was naked at the same time. His eyes dropped to her breasts and widened. They rose to her face again and his concern had been replaced by desire. An answering twinge of heat rose inside her.

With Bianca's delicious naked body in his arms, Loki simply couldn't resist her any longer. He leaned forward and brushed his lips across her mouth questioningly. Instead of pulling away, she went still. He kissed her again, nipping at her lips until she opened her mouth. When she did, he slid his tongue inside. She started and her small hands tightened on his shoulders. Slowly and carefully so he didn't frighten her, he deepened their kiss.

Sean hadn't been very experienced and he hadn't had Loki's skill. Just his lips on hers was enough to have Bianca quivering inside. His shoulders were wide and his skin was silky beneath her palms. She ran her hands down to his chest and he groaned into her mouth. "I love it when you touch me," he breathed, then kissed her again.

Emboldened, she explored his muscular body and ran her fingers down to his abs. His stomach tightened and he thrust his tongue into her mouth. It was too much of a reminder of what Sean had done to her and she tried to pull away.

Realizing he'd frightened her, he shifted his mouth to her jaw and pressed soft kisses along it until he reached her ear. "I promise I won't hurt you," he said in a low voice that made her insides melt. "Let me show you pleasure unlike anything you've ever felt before." He drew back to see her eyes had changed color again. They were now pale blue with desire.

Caught in Loki's gaze, Bianca could barely think. Her body was crying out for what he promised her, but her mind remembered how much it had hurt last time. He stroked a hand down her back again and his touch was gentle. Ashley's words floated into her head. What harm could there be in finding temporary enjoyment? Maybe sex with Loki wouldn't be as bad as it had been with Sean. "Okay," she said in a croak.

Triumph blazed inside Loki. He wanted to crush Bianca to his chest and devour her, but he forced himself to be gentle. Standing, he carried her to the pile of clothing she'd laid out to dry on the ground. He sat her down and stripped off his clothes. Her eyes went to his obvious desire and she gulped in fear and drew her legs up to her chest.

Seeing Loki in all of his naked glory, Bianca was reminded of how small she was when he knelt in front of her. She couldn't tear her eyes away from his erection. Sean had just been a boy when he'd taken her virginity. The Asgardian was most definitely a man and she was convinced that he was going to hurt her.

Putting his fingers beneath Bianca's chin, Loki tilted her head back until she met his eyes. At his mental order, the light dimmed, throwing them into shadow. "Do you trust me?" he asked.

Breathing shallowly, she jerked her head in a nod. They'd been companions for a few weeks now and he'd proven he was trustworthy. "What do you want me to do?" she asked.

"I want you on my lap again," he said and sat next to her. She hesitantly let him shift her so she was straddling him. He perused her body and closed his eyes for a few seconds. "I've been picturing you naked from the moment we met, but my imagination did not do you justice."

Beads of water were scattered all over her body. One hung from the tip of her breast. Leaning down, he licked it off and she made a small sound of surprise. Her hands went to his shoulders again as he gently caught her nipple between his teeth. He sucked her into his mouth and her hips jerked towards him instinctively.

Loki's hands slid down her body to her hips and he lifted her up so she was on her knees. Now he didn't have to bend down so far to reach her breasts. He kept one hand on her hip and let the other roam over her body. Dragging his mouth from her breasts up to her mouth, he kissed her as he fondled her breast. "It is almost as if you were made for me," he whispered.

He lay her down on her side, then rolled her over until she was on her back. He loomed over her and horrible memories assailed her once more. She put her hands on his chest and made a sound of protest. Backing away slightly, he rained kisses on her jaw, then worked his way down her neck to her breasts.

Savage rage flowed through Loki that she had to battle her fear before she could allow him to show her pleasure. He wanted to find the boy who had hurt her and tear him limb from limb. Instead, he focused on turning her fear into wonder.

The sensation of Loki's mouth on her breasts and his large hands sliding up and down her body relaxed Bianca. He swept a hand down her leg and inserted it between her knees. At his gentle nudging, she allowed him to push her legs apart just enough for him to slide his hand up to the apex of her thighs. He left it there so his fingers were resting against her most sensitive area, but he didn't attempt to invade her.

Her breasts were throbbing as he worked his way down to her navel. He brushed a fingertip against her core and a small sound escaped her. Her legs widened fractionally and he rubbed her again. She didn't realize why he was sliding down her body until his tongue replaced his finger. With a moan of pure need, she allowed him to spread her legs apart. Hot and wet, his tongue quickly worked her into a frenzy. She'd never felt anything like this before, except in a dream. This time, she was going to feel the pleasure that had been stolen from her when she'd been woken by the clones.

Loki held himself in check when Bianca writhed beneath him. Her hands were tangled in his hair as he worked her to the edge of ecstasy with his mouth. His need became too great to ignore and he made his way back up her body. Before she could tense up, he nudged his way into her. She was almost too small to take him, but her body was ready for him and he slid himself inside her. "Are you all right?" he asked hoarsely. To say it was a tight fit would be an understatement.

Feeling him fully sheathed inside her, she was amazed that there was no pain. He was much bigger than Sean had been, but it didn't feel like he was tearing her apart. "Yes," she said breathlessly, then moaned when he pulled back and slid into her again. Her moans increased as he set a slow, steady pace. The pleasure that had almost crested before quickly built up again.

Loki allowed himself a smug smile as Bianca began to tighten around him already. She was easily the smallest woman he'd ever had the pleasure of bedding. He couldn't pound himself into her the way he longed to. That would have to wait until after she'd become accustomed to him. As it was, he had to take exquisite care not to hurt her as he thrust deeply into her.

He knew she was near the edge when her breaths came in short, sharp pants. She moaned his name and her short fingernails bit into his back. Her hips rose to meet his, working faster and faster until he lost control. Calling her name, he felt her contracting around him as he speared into her deeply and reached his climax.

Head spinning from sheer pleasure, Bianca was dazed when Loki rolled off her. He brushed her hair back from her forehead and his expression was tender. "Did I hurt you?" he asked.

Assessing her body, she shook her head. "No. That was…" She didn't have words to describe the sensations that had assailed her.

"I believe 'spectacular' is the word you're looking for," he said smugly. "I agree. That was very pleasurable." In fact, he couldn't wait to get her naked again. If she hadn't been so new to sex, he would have spent the entire night making love to her. She was bound to be sore in the morning, so he regretfully decided further pleasure would have to wait.

Chapter Forty

They rinsed off before dressing, then returned to the campfire. Mack eyed them both suspiciously and gave Bianca a disapproving look when she lay down. "What?" she whispered crankily. "I'm an adult. I can have sex if I want to."

He rolled his eyes, then turned and bared his teeth at Loki, who sniggered in response. Zan opened one eye, took in what they'd been up to and closed it again. Ashley was the only one who woke the next morning unaware of what had happened. She figured out that something had happened quickly enough by the awkward way everyone was behaving. "What did I miss?" she asked after a far too silent breakfast. Loki was watching Bianca with a self-satisfied grin and she was avoiding his gaze completely.

"They had sex," Zan said and Bianca choked on her tea.

"It's about time," Ashley said with a grin. "The sexual tension was getting a bit much to bear."

Bianca sputtered in indignation. "You two are just as bad!" she said accusingly and the teens looked everywhere but at each other. "Why don't you go and have sex so there won't be any more sexual tension for any of us to suffer through?"

"That's a great idea," Ashley said. Hell, if Bianca had relaxed enough to let Loki get her naked, why shouldn't she and Zan take the time to get better acquainted? "Coming?" she said to Zan and headed for the tunnel to the spring.

Zan hesitated long enough for Loki to conjure a magic globe for him, then he hurried after her. He almost tripped over his own feet in his haste to catch up to her. Ashley's giggle floated back to them, then the sound faded with distance.

"Since we're alone," Loki said and lifted an eyebrow suggestively.

"We aren't alone," Bianca said flatly and pointed at Mack. The monkey wore a grouchy expression and sat with his arms crossed, glaring at Loki.

"Do you regret what we did last night?" he asked. His moods were mercurial and he was suddenly serious.

Bianca hadn't slept well due to the memories of pleasure that had assailed her all night. "No," she replied. "But one bout of sex doesn't make us a couple."

He blinked, then grinned lopsidedly. "Finally, I've met a woman just like me. Sex without any emotional attachments is right up my alley." He winked, but she couldn't shake the feeling it was just a front. Surely, he didn't think there could ever be anything between them. Her lifespan would be the blink of an eye for him. She would grow old and die while he would remain young and handsome for eons.

Loki hid his hurt behind a carefree façade. He knew their relationship would be temporary, but he'd expected her to at least care about him in some small way. She'd sounded so cold that he could hardly believe she'd been moaning and writhing beneath him last night. He couldn't wait to repeat the experience and she seemed not to care either way.

Ashley and Zan finally returned several hours later. Arm in arm, they looked deliriously happy. Loki flicked them a sullen look, then grabbed Zan's bow. While he'd finally managed to seduce Bianca, she was pretending they were strangers now. He stalked off to hunt, preferring solitude for a while.

"What's wrong with him?" Ashley asked, watching the Asgardian's rapidly receding back.

"He thinks Bianca doesn't care for him the same way he cares for her," Zan said wisely. "He's wrong, of course, but he's too stubborn to see it." Bianca's expression turned mulish. "I think they are both as stubborn as each other," he added.

Ashley looked at their diminutive leader and shook her head sadly. "You know you care about him. Why would you let him think you don't?"

"Because he's going to leave," Bianca said wearily. "I don't want to do something stupid like fall for him when he has no intention of staying here."

"You could go with him," Ashley suggested.

"Where? To Ass Guard?" Bianca snorted out a laugh. "You've seen what he thinks of us. I'm sure all Asgardians think of humans as a lesser species. I'm just a lowly mortal, not a god like him." Her tone was bitter and reflected her anguish. She could possibly learn to love a man like Loki, but he would never love someone like her. While she might occasionally share her body with him, she was determined to keep her heart locked up safe.

Instead of leaving the cave to hunt, Zan remained with the girls and Mack. Ashley was sewing more clothes for them and Bianca was doing her best to help. Zan could sew to some extent, but he wasn't very neat. He was just happy to have a beautiful girlfriend and Bianca for his friend. He was even getting used to the strange monkey.

Sensing Bianca's mood was low, Mack gave up on shunning her and climbed up to her shoulder. He snuggled against her neck in silent apology for ignoring her. She knew he was worried she would grow to care more about Loki than she did about him. Pulling him into her arms, she held him against her chest like a baby and patted his back. His small arms went around her neck and his tail curled around her arm. This was how she used to hold him when she'd first begun to animate him. It had become a comfort for them both.

"Where did you find Mack?" Ashley asked. Bianca didn't talk about her past much and she was still an enigma.

"In a city called Reaverton," she replied. Both teens gasped at the dire name. "Before the invasion, it was just a normal city, or so I've been told. Reavers came after the apocalypse."

Zan shuddered slightly at the ill-named city. "I couldn't imagine an entire city full of reavers."

"I could," Ashley said darkly and he put an arm around her shoulders.

"It was the first scavenging trip that Tran Li took me on," Bianca told them. "I found a bunch of toys and Mack was at the bottom of the pile. He only had one eye and he looked so forlorn that I couldn't leave him behind."

"Did my uncle see you animate him?" Zan asked.

She shook her head ruefully. "He knew I could use magic, but I rarely used it in front of him because I knew it made him nervous. I practiced bringing Mack to life when I was alone."

"You were so lucky Zan's uncle saved you from the droids and clones," Ashley said.

"It was his destiny," Zan insisted. "Everything happens for a reason. Even the apocalypse."

"What possible reason could there be for the Earth to have been destroyed?" Bianca asked.

"Ah, but the planet was not destroyed," he responded wisely. "Mankind was driven to the brink of extinction, but we survived, as did some of the plants and animals. The Viltarans might have wiped out every other civilization they encountered, but they were not quite able to annihilate us. If the rumors are true, the soldiers are planning to fight back and reclaim control of our world from our enemies."

"There are still far more droids and clones than us," Bianca said. "I don't see how we could possibly kill them all."

"You will find a way," he said with absolute faith in her.

"Me?" she said skeptically. "Don't you mean the soldiers will find a way?"

"I doubt it," he said with a half-shrug. "I believe you will be the spearhead of this war. You will be instrumental in our victory."

"What about Loki?" Ashley asked. "He's even more powerful than Bianca."

"This is not his world," Zan said with a hint of sadness. "His destiny lies elsewhere."

The ache in Bianca's chest told her he was right. Loki might be with them for a while, but it wasn't his job to save this planet. What her friends didn't realize was that she didn't care what happened to their world. She didn't want to become a champion. She just wanted a life that wasn't filled with horror and danger.

Chapter Forty-One

Glad to have some time alone, Loki strode away from the cave. He wasn't sure why he was so annoyed by Bianca's cavalier attitude. After some thought, he realized it irked him that she wasn't as drawn to him as he was to her.

He brooded about the pathway his life had taken as he went in search of food. Odin's punishment to banish him from Asgard had been harsher than he'd probably intended. There was a very good chance that he might die on this godforsaken planet. It was doubtful Heimdall could see into this dimension to check up on him. His kin might never know the trials that he would suffer through. Then again, they probably wouldn't care. In fact, they would be glad to get rid of him permanently.

His mood worsened as he trudged through the increasingly hot wasteland. He spied a rattlesnake and flicked a dagger at it, severing its head. It left a trail of blood beside him as he gripped it by the tail and continued on.

He'd collected several snakes and one coyote when he saw movement overhead. He tilted his head back to see a vulture lazily circling him. Seeing slightly mussed feathers on its right wing, he sucked in a breath. He could have sworn it was the same one he'd spied back near Reaverton and several other places along their journey. There always seemed to be vultures wherever they went, but surely they didn't follow people this far across the desert?

His intuition told him there was something very strange about this bird. Easing the coyote and snakes from his shoulder to the ground, he readied his bow and drew an arrow from the quiver. Setting it in place, he pretended to aim for something ahead and waited for the vulture to glide into his view again. When it was directly above him, he aimed upwards and let fly. The bird made an alarmed buzzing noise that wasn't at all natural when the projectile hit it. The arrow had lodged in its belly, but it didn't fall from the sky. Instead, it flapped its wings and beat a hasty retreat.

"That is not a real bird," he said out loud. Disturbed by what he'd just discovered, he gathered his food and headed back to the caverns.

Bianca and Mack were the only ones sitting near the banked fire when he entered. "Where are Ashley and Zan?" he asked.

"They're at the spring," she replied. "They're having some more…private time."

He knew that meant they were having sex. "Good. I don't want them to hear this just yet."

Intrigued, she watched his tense face as he put the snakes and coyote down and sat next to her. "What happened?" she asked. He didn't have any visible injuries, so he probably hadn't been attacked by droids or raiders.

"I just saw a vulture that seems to be following us. I'm pretty sure it's the same one I saw back in Reaverton and several more times since then."

"Vultures don't follow prey that far," she protested, being careful to keep her voice down so it didn't carry.

"This bird isn't what it seems," he said. "I shot it with an arrow and it didn't die. It made a strange noise, then flew off."

"What sort of noise?"

"An almost metallic buzzing sound."

"You mean like a droid that's been injured?"

He nodded and they stared at each other, trying to figure out what this meant. "Did the Viltarans make bird, or animal robots?" Loki asked.

"Not as far as I know. They only made the nine-foot-tall ones."

"Then who made the vulture and set it to spy on us?"

"No one even knows who you really are," she pointed out. "It might have been left to spy on my family."

"You're probably right," he conceded. "The invaders would want to make sure no other witches came from the Caldwell line."

"If it's been watching me this whole time, it has to know that I can use magic."

"It probably also knows that I can use magic by now," he added. "Someone has to be in charge of the vulture. Perhaps the droids have a mechanical overlord."

"It could be tracking us so it can send some robots to ambush us."

"That is what I would do," Loki concurred. "In which case, we need to reach the soldiers before the metal men can catch up to us." Unlike them, the droids didn't have to rest. They might be slow, but they could still cover a lot of ground. They might be closer than they knew and they could appear at any time.

"We have to let Ashley and Zan know about this," Bianca said.

"Know about what?" Zan asked as he and his new girlfriend sauntered into view. Their hair was dripping and their faces were flushed. It was easy to tell what they'd been up to.

Ashley's happy grin faded at their grim expressions. "What's going on?" she demanded.

Loki described the robotic bird that had been following them and the theory he and Bianca had come up with.

"We need to leave," Zan surmised. "We don't want to become penned inside the cavern."

"Aren't we going to wait until nightfall?" Ashley asked. She didn't relish the idea of walking through the blistering heat.

"It's too dangerous for us to stay here any longer," Bianca said. "If there is a droid army coming for us, the longer we stay in one place, the more danger we'll be in."

"The soldiers are our best hope of finding safety," Loki added. He'd seen the disintegrating ray guns the metal men used. Whatever defenses the soldiers had erected wouldn't last long against them. But they might slow them down long enough to mount an attack.

Working quickly, Bianca and Ashley butchered the coyote and snakes. Loki roasted them while Zan packed up their gear. Mack was hunched on Bianca's shoulder, holding onto her and shivering in fear. He made small, whimpering noises every now and then that she could do nothing to soothe.

Ashley had sewn two sheets of canvass together to act as a cover in the event that they were ever forced to walk through the heat of the day. Glad for her foresight, now she took the lead and held up one end while Loki brought up the rear and held the other. The ground was already baking beneath their feet, but at least they were hidden under the shade.

Their backpacks were heavy with dried meat, water and assorted gear. Bianca carried much more than she would have been able to previously. She didn't know why her strength had increased so much and she was a little afraid of the changes that were happening to her. In another few months, she would turn twenty-one. With that milestone, there was a good chance her magic would receive another boost. That surely had to be the reason for the changes.

They kept a constant vigil as they trekked back towards the train tracks that would guide them to their destination. The vulture remained absent and Loki couldn't see anything moving in the distance in any direction. If the droids were coming for them, they were still too far away for him to see. Or maybe they were deliberately staying out of sight and were waiting for the opportunity to sneak up on them when they were sleeping.

Bianca had the same thought and spoke. "We should take turns keeping watch whenever we rest from now on."

"I agree," Loki said. While Ashley had to switch arms to hold the canvas up, his weren't even tired yet. "We can't allow ourselves to become vulnerable," he added.

Zan voiced a question that had been playing on his mind ever since he'd learned who Bianca was. "Are you going to tell the soldiers the truth about yourself?"

"I'm not sure that would be a very good idea," Bianca replied. "People have a tendency to try to kill me when they learn I can use magic."

"It might be best for us to pretend to be simple civilians," Loki added. Mack sent him a grumpy look, knowing this meant he would have to play dead whenever they had company.

"How long will you be able to get away with that?" Ashley said doubtfully. "Someone will find out sooner or later. They might not be happy that we kept it from them."

"We'll cross that bridge when we get to it," Bianca decided. She shuddered to think what the soldiers would do once they figured out who and what she was. With luck, they would see her as an ally. Worst case scenario, they might hand them over to the very droids they were fleeing from in the hopes that their town would be spared from an attack.

Chapter Forty-Two

They stopped a couple of hours before dark and had a quick meal. Ashley and Zan shared a bedroll and fell into an exhausted sleep. They hadn't bothered to erect a tent. Their rest would be brief before they would continue on.

"I will keep watch," Loki offered. He spoke quietly so he wouldn't wake the teens.

"I'm not tired," Bianca replied just as quietly.

He studied her face and saw a hint of gray in her eyes. "What is troubling you?" he asked. Gray meant she was feeling down and he wanted to know why.

"Ashley and Zan are in danger because of me," she said in a low voice. "I've drawn them into my problems and they could die because of it."

"They will eventually die anyway," he said philosophically. "I imagine the average life expectancy is quite young on this world." Most people he'd seen so far hadn't been older than their forties. Malnutrition and lack of water was one cause. Being hunted by droids and clones was another. "Besides," he added, "their lives have been vastly improved since they joined our merry band."

She uttered a short, skeptical snort. "Improved how, exactly?"

"They have plenty of food and water and they've found companionship in each other," he replied. "Is that not better than being forced to live as a raider, or spending their entire lives alone?"

"Maybe. But I can't shake the feeling that we're heading into danger."

"We will always be in danger," he pointed out. "There is no place on this world that could truly be safe from the droids and clones." Not to mention the people who had turned rogue. They were just as bad as the invaders who had ruined this planet.

Mack gently tugged on Bianca's hair to get her attention and pointed over her shoulder. She turned to see Zan had protectively put his arm around Ashley in his sleep. It was obvious the pair cared about each other already. She felt a moment of bitter jealousy before stifling the emotion. While Loki desired her, he could never love her. No one would. She was considered to be a freak on this world. With luck, she might find a way to leave when he did and find a place where she could belong.

Loki noted the sadness that flickered over Bianca's face before her expression went blank. She was an outsider and was reviled by her own people. They were the same in that respect. They could also both use magic. Their similarities were startling when he thought about it. His father had reportedly raped his mother and she'd left her servants to raise him. He'd grown up feeling alone and unloved, just as Bianca had after her mother had been murdered. Neither of them could truly trust anyone else. They would always be waiting for treachery of some kind. The only difference between them was that she was mortal and he would outlive her by thousands of years.

For a moment, he almost wished he was a mortal as well. He imagined growing old with Bianca and raising children with her. His mouth twisted in a bitter smile as reality came crashing down. Both of his marriages had ended badly, one in death and the other in divorce. Now that he'd been exiled from Asgard, his offspring would no doubt hate him even more than they already had. In their eyes, he was a failure. He wasn't a father that they could be proud of.

Sensing Loki's melancholy mood, Bianca didn't have the skill to draw him out of it. Tran Li had preferred silence to conversation. Small talk wasn't something she'd learned to engage in after years of neglect as a child.

Seeing something streak through the sky as the last rays of sunlight died, her hands jerked towards her daggers. They stilled when she realized it was just a shooting star. If the vulture made a return, she was going to do her best to disable it permanently. An arrow hadn't even slowed it down, but her daggers might have more luck.

"What are you thinking about?" Loki asked when he saw a smile playing around Bianca's mouth. It had been almost cruel rather than amused, which intrigued him.

"If I see that vulture again, I'm going to introduce it to my daggers." She patted the weapons and they quivered for a moment.

"You should name them," he suggested. "They are alive, after all. In a fashion anyway."

It had never occurred to her to name them and she drew a blank. "What am I supposed to call them? Human names wouldn't really suit deadly weapons."

"Hmm," Loki mused. "How about Amun and Ra?"

"What are the origins of those names?"

"They were Egyptian gods. Amun was the god of wind and Ra was the sun god. Combined, they became Amun-Ra, the most powerful god of all at the time."

"Were they real?"

He lifted a shoulder and let it drop. "They existed long before I was born. They were already largely a myth when I learned of them when I visited Earth."

Bianca's smile was more genuine this time as she pulled her daggers. She addressed the left one first. "I'm going to call you Amun." She turned to the right one next. "You're Ra. Together, you are Amun-Ra."

The daggers seemed to contemplate their new names before saluting her with their pointed hilts.

"I think they like their new names," Loki said in a pleased tone as she slid them back into their sheaths.

"You get a kick out of naming them after long dead gods, don't you?" Bianca said dryly.

His teeth were very white in the encroaching darkness when he smiled. "I do," he confessed. "I have always been perverse."

"That doesn't surprise me at all."

"What were you like as a child?" he queried. He knew she'd had a tough life, but he wanted to know more about her.

"Do you really want to know about my childhood?" she replied skeptically. He arched a brow, clearly unwilling to let the subject drop, so she huffed out a sigh. "I was only six when my mother died. No one wanted to take care of me afterwards, so I had to live on the scraps of food I found around the campfires when no one was looking."

Indignation and rage rose inside Loki at her ill treatment. He crossed his arms, grasped his biceps and ground his teeth together so he wouldn't break into her story. He'd asked her to recount her past and now he would sit quietly and hear it.

"I already told you the other kids used to taunt me," she went on and he nodded. His jaw was clenched and his eyes were icy. "I had to hide from them during the day so they wouldn't gang up on me and beat me up," she explained. "Sean was the only one who never abused me."

Loki could no longer hold his silence. "He waited until you were fourteen before he did that," he said bitterly.

Ignoring his outburst, she drew her legs up to her chest and wrapped her arms around them. Mack snuggled against her neck and curled his arms and tail around her to offer her comfort. "Craig caught me alone one day when I was thirteen," she said. She was speaking barely above a whisper now, but he didn't have to strain to hear her. "He looked me up and down, realizing I wasn't a child anymore I guess. He said I looked exactly like my mother and that I would turn out to be a whore just like her."

Her whole body was tense when Loki placed a hand on her back. "How did you react to that?" he asked.

"I always knew he hated me," she replied with a haunted look, but with no signs of tears. "There was so much loathing in his eyes that I knew he wanted to kill me. After that, I tried to be very careful not to use my magic at all. If he'd seen me use it, he wouldn't have hesitated to execute me."

"I bet he jumped at the chance to exile you once Sean ran to tattle on you," Loki said.

"They came for me as soon as he started shouting," she said and shivered. Loki shifted closer to lend her his body warmth. "I didn't get far before they caught me. They tied me up and wrapped material around my eyes so I couldn't see. They tossed me into the back of the cart and took me to Reaverton, then tied me to the pole. One of them yanked the blindfold off so I could see my end coming." She was silent for a while as she replayed the events in her mind. "I was sure I was going to die when the sun went down and I heard a clone roar. Then Tran Li came out of the darkness, as silent as a shadow. He cut me loose and took me away before the droids or clones even knew we were there."

"I wish he was still alive," Loki said huskily and hugged her to his side. "I think I would have liked him."

"He would have hated you," Bianca said with a fond smile.

"Why?" he asked indignantly.

"Because you're a stranger," she explained. "It took him a few weeks to warm up to me."

"I wonder if that is because he lost his entire family," he mused. "It would have been hard to adjust to having a strange young girl come into his life." Especially one who was so emotionally damaged. Discovering she could use magic would have been even harder for a lone man to accept. She was lucky he hadn't just walked away. "Did he ever tell you why he saved you?" he queried.

"He said that all life is precious and that murder was abhorrent to him. Leaving me to die would have been the same as if he'd killed me himself. I was too young and unskilled to survive, so he felt obligated to train me. Over time, I think he came to care for me. It was hard to tell with him, though."

"If he was as inscrutable as young Zan tends to be, I can understand what you mean," he said dryly. She flashed him a smile and he became very conscious of her luscious body next to his. Mack sent him a cool look, as if he could sense where his thoughts were straying. With a mental sigh, he withdrew his arm from her shoulder and stood. "The lovebirds have rested for long enough," he said and offered her his hand. "We should get moving."

Grasping Loki's hand, Bianca allowed him to pull her to her feet. She was surprised she'd told him so much about her history. Maybe she was getting used to being around other people again. Having friends was a new phenomenon to her. It was one she thought she could get used to, but she had to remind herself not to rely on them. Doing so could only end in disappointment.

Chapter Forty-Three

As Zan had predicted, it took them roughly three weeks to reach the mysterious city that was run by soldiers. High metal walls should have shone brightly beneath the afternoon sun when they were close enough for all of them to see it. Instead, they were almost invisible. The soldiers had painted them a sandy brown color to blend in with the wasteland.

Loki spotted the city long before the others saw it. A bad feeling rose inside him at first sight of it. Even from a distance, he could tell these humans were far more organized and prepared than the ones he'd met so far. Armed men with hard faces kept watch in all directions. Their guns were ancient, but he was willing to bet they were in good working order. Some even carried the disintegrating weapons that had been stripped from fallen droids.

"Are we sure we really want to do this?" Ashley asked nervously as the guards spotted them. Shouts were heard from within the settlement. It was a far larger city than the one Silvia had taken over.

"It is our destiny," Zan said with infuriating calm. "We were led here for a reason that will become clear in time."

Bianca flicked a look at Loki to see his expression was just as skeptical as hers. "Remember our story," she said.

"We know," Ashley said wearily. It had been repeated so often by now that she could recite it in her sleep. "We're survivors from a cave that was attacked by raiders. We were searching for another cavern when we met some people who mentioned this town. It seemed the safest place for us, so we came searching for it."

Bianca nodded and nervously wiped sweaty hands on her pants. Mack was riding in her backpack. He would remain in there unless she told him it was safe. She wouldn't draw her daggers unless it became absolutely necessary. It went without saying that she and Loki wouldn't display their ability to use magic.

Moving slowly and keeping their hands out to show they meant no harm, they closed in on the town. A gate that looked like part of the wall opened and twenty men and women moved to surround them. Their expressions were flat and their eyes were emotionless. They would pull the trigger without hesitation and without remorse.

A man with dark blond hair that was kept cropped close to his head strode forward. His face was craggy and a scar ran across his chin. He was average height and on the stocky side. Green eyes took them in, examining them closely as he assessed whether they posed a danger. "I am Major Lincoln," he said. "Who are you and what do you want?"

It had been agreed that Loki would be their spokesperson. As the oldest male in their group, they would expect him to be in charge. "We are simple civilians," he said, using a fake accent to blend in. He gave the major the spiel they'd rehearsed. "We are just looking for somewhere safe from droids and clones," he finished up with a winning smile.

Lincoln nodded thoughtfully, then dashed their hopes when he spoke. "That's quite a story you've concocted. Unfortunately for you, my bullshit meter is telling me it's a pack of lies."

"Fine," Bianca said tightly. "Don't believe us. We'll just be on our way then."

"I don't think so," the major said and his unit cocked their weapons. "You're not going anywhere until I learn the truth." He made a curt gesture and two more men appeared. They stripped their weapons from them and took their backpacks as well.

Loki's illusion hid his sword and daggers, but he was seething that their ruse had failed. Instead of being welcomed with open arms, they'd been greeted with suspicion and deadly weapons. The major motioned for them to get moving and they had no choice but to obey. If he or Bianca used even a flicker of magic, they would open fire and shred them to pieces.

Ashley and Zan clasped hands as they were marched through the gates. Like Ashley's previous temporary home among the raiders, the buildings were mostly made of metal that had been scrounged from the derelict oil fields.

They were split up and soldiers escorted their captives to separate cells in different buildings. They clearly weren't going to give them a chance to talk and come up with a new story. Bianca mentally cursed as she was shoved inside a small, dark room. A metal cot with a thin mattress was attached to one wall. A bucket in a corner would serve as her toilet. There were no facilities to wash with, which came as no surprise.

Taking a seat on the cot, she tried not to fall into despair. Now that they'd been separated, she had no way of knowing what was happening to her friends. The major didn't seem like he would have much patience if they continued to lie to him. She was left with the horrible choice of sacrificing herself, or letting her new friends suffer.

Her tension mounted as she was left to stew in the cell alone. A guard stood watch beside the metal door that had a glassless window and thick bars. He glanced inside every now and then to make sure she wasn't trying anything. She gave a mirthless laugh at that. Everything was made of metal, except the mattress. There was nothing she could use as a weapon or a tool to try to escape. At least as far as they knew. With her talents, she could probably devise a way to free herself fairly easily.

Eventually, the outer door opened and Major Lincoln strode inside. He nodded at the guard, who unlocked the cell. Stepping into the room, he placed a metal chair down, then sat. He regarded Bianca silently and she stared back at him. It was almost like being with Tran Li again. She smiled a little and he narrowed his eyes. "Do you find something amusing?" he asked in a stern tone.

"You remind me of someone," she replied. "His name was Tran Li."

"Who was he?"

"He was my friend and mentor. He was Zan's uncle, but they were separated seven years ago."

He regarded her in silence for a while. "Your friends are refusing to tell me anything, but you seem to be more willing to talk. Why is that?"

Bianca took a deep breath, then let it out. "They're protecting me."

"From who?"

"From you and your men. As soon as I tell you who I am, you'll probably try to kill me."

His lips thinned. "And why is that?"

"My name is Bianca Caldwell," she told him with as much calm as she could muster. "I'm Whitney

Caldwell's great-grand daughter and I'm a witch just like she was."

His eyes widened and he moved so fast that she didn't have time to react. He pulled his handgun, but instead of shooting her, he hit her in the temple with the butt. Darkness came crashing down, bringing dread and hopelessness with it. As consciousness faded, she hoped she'd managed to save Loki and her friends with her confession. With her luck, she'd probably just doomed them all to death.

Printed in Great Britain
by Amazon